SIR FRANCIS CHANTREY
By George Jones, R.A.

Fly-Fishing
Fact vs. Fiction

Fly-Fishing

Fact vs. Fiction

Jo Rippier

COLIN SMYTHE LIMITED

First published by Colin Smythe Limited
38 Mill Lane, Gerrards Cross, Buckinghamshire SL9 8BA
www.colinsmythe.co.uk

The right of Jo Rippier to be identified as the Author of this work
has been asserted in accordance with Sections 77 and 78
of the Copyright, Designs and Patents Act, 1988

British Library Cataloguing-in-Publication Data
A catalogue record for this book
is available from the British Library

ISBN: 978-0-86140-499-5

Produced in Great Britain
Typeset by Pageset Ltd, High Wycombe, Buckinghamshire
Printed and bound by CPI Antony Rowe Ltd, Chippenham, Wiltshire

For
Malcolm Greenhalgh
in gratitude for so many fishing days together –
either two, or three men in a boat.

Acknowledgement and gratitude here expressed for permission to re-print *Fine & Far Off* to Verlag: J. Schück Publishers, Nürnberg, Germany.

This little book is partly an attempt, through the medium of seemingly random reflections, to catch moments in a long life when what happens is never forgotten. But it is also a reference to ways in which a lifelong passion may find means of expressing itself in rather unexpected directions.

Contents

TRIALS OF A NOVICE

Angler. "Hush! Keep *back!* Keep *back!* I had **a**
beautiful rise just then; shall get **another** directly."

I

One Thing Leads To Another

This is really as much a story of friendship as of fishing. And it started nearly fifty years ago. It was my second year in Germany. It was also summer. I said to myself "I am going to catch a trout today." This was actually pushing things, as at the time I knew of nowhere where I might go in expectation of fulfilling such a wish.

I took out a map and started looking for likely possibilities. North of Frankfurt there was a range of mountains. On the other side of those mountains I suddenly noticed thin blue lines, which could only be streams.

I must admit straight away that having decided I would catch a fish, it was also obvious to me that in order to do so, I would have to poach. This could turn out to be an interesting activity since, if caught, I would be guilty not only of an angling offence, but also of having fished without a licence.

I set off.

As I came down the other side of the mountains, I suddenly found myself actually driving beside a very trouty-looking stream. It was also very beautiful countryside, wooded, undulating, almost pristine. Things were definitely looking up. However I still had to make the first move. I continued driving for a number of kilometres without being able to decide where I was to start making trouble for myself.

And then, as I came over the top of a slight incline, I suddenly saw two anglers in a field beside the stream. "Hm, no harm in asking," I thought, "they can only say no."

I stopped the car, and walked towards the two figures. As I came nearer, one of them abruptly turned round and started walking fast in the other direction. I approached and asked the angler facing me what my chances might be.

"You'd better ask him!" he said, pointing in the direction of the other angler.

I rushed on, finally catching up with the other fisherman who in the meanwhile was standing at the side of the stream. He turned as I started to speak, listened to my request and then addressed the following questions to me:

"Are you English?" I nodded.

"Are you a fly fisherman?" I nodded again.

"Well, this is a Hardy rod. See what you can do with it," he said, pointing towards the stream.

It really must have been my lucky day, as with that first cast I hooked a trout. One of the many to be caught in the years that followed. The result of that first meeting was an invitation to meet the rest of the family, a friendship which was to last until a few years ago when Hubertus died. That friendship with a wonderful family has been one of the great high points of my stay in Germany, and also later led to fishing on another river, the Eder, which was, for thirty years, a paradise.

The Weil, on the banks of which I met Hubertus, was to remain a regular venue for many years. Most of the fish were wild browns, occasionally joined by rainbows which strayed from stocked stretches further down. And for a small stream it occasionally offered chances of taking fish of surprising size. I will not forget one brown trout of 2 ½ lb which I discovered late one September afternoon.

But there was a rainbow I will also not forget. It was a little over two pounds and had taken up residence in a small wooded pool. I fished for that fish. How I fished for that fish. It rose to my flies on a number of occasions. Somehow I could not get it to stay on. Until one day when it did.

That day remained with me for another reason. I had parked my car on a path leading down to the stream. When I had finished fishing, I got into the car and tried to start it. Nothing happened.

At that very moment a young man out walking passed my car. He noticed my difficulties and asked if he could help. He just happened to be a Volkswagen mechanic! He solved my problem. I invited him for a meal at the restaurant at the top of the slope, and even gave him the rainbow trout which I had caught. It was a most fortunate turn of events.

There were also chub in some of the pools which actually were more difficult to catch on the fly than trout. I was highly amused to discover that the best way of inducing them to take was to cast not ahead of them, but at their tails. They would then, if in the mood, swing round and grab the fly.

Today I have that Hardy rod I had put in my hands at our first meeting. It was left to me in Hubertus' will. A most touching reminder of a wonderful and lasting friendship.

Red Letter Day

Serendipity is a wonderful word conjuring up all kinds of magical associations, none of which are easily put into words. Nevertheless it was the random reading of a book, *Fishing for Seatrout* (H.P. Henzell, 1949) which gave me ideas for flies for loch fishing on South Uist. One such, The Seagull, which I had never even heard of, initially aroused mild amusement until it actually provoked a rise from a good-sized sea trout, subsequently landed.

Another fly mentioned in passing by Henzell, Red Palmer, also stimulated my imagination, and eventually added additional meaning to the title of this little piece. Before going any further, a small passing thought. As in cooking, most people consciously or unconsciously make small changes, even if they think they are sticking scrupulously to the recipe. In referring back to the book, I discovered that I had inadvertently altered something. The original tying could not have been simpler, or clearer: red seal-fur body and red hackle, palmered.

I had discovered among my collection of capes one which was striking, and almost violently crimson. I made up some Red Palmers using hackle from this cape. For some strange reason, instead of tying a red body, I used peacock herl. Interestingly enough Henzell, though mentioning the Red Palmer, also adapted and seemed keener on his Bronze Spider, which apparently also caught him fish. I quote "… but why sea trout take it, unless the shine on the moving hackle attracts them, I do not know: let it suffice that they do."

On one of the days conditions did not seem propitious. It was bright, with not a murmur of breeze disturbing the surface of the loch. We tried initially with the usual three wet flies. Nothing moved. The loch seemed not only dour but lifeless. We switched to dry fly. A Daddy Longlegs on the bob and, just for the fun of it, a small Red Palmer on the tail. We had sea trout on both flies. Sometimes rather explosive rises.

The last day brought with it almost gale-force winds. Malcolm, my partner in the boat, decided to go home, as it was obviously going to be difficult for two to fish properly in a boat whizzing down the loch. For reasons I cannot explain, I decided to put on the bob a long-shanked size 10 Red Palmer. Ian Kennedy, our long-suffering boatman looked at the Red Palmer, and then glanced heavenwards. He said nothing. I said nothing. In fact we continued the silence for quite some time. I could sense Ian's unhappiness with that bob-fly which skittered merrily along the surface, sending crimson beams in all directions. Ian's disapproval was actually quite understandable. He has spent his whole life on the island and is an outstandingly brilliant and innovative angler. Compared with him, visitors are mere casuals.

But then it happened.

Something one dreams of, but also envisions with apprehension. A huge shape emerged from the white-topped waves, rose, and went down. Ian and I both froze. A very big fish. What's more, it was attached to the Red Palmer. And for once nothing went wrong. After not very long, a beautiful fresh sea trout was swung into the boat – a fraction under seven pounds. The fish of a lifetime.

In retrospect one wonders what provoked that fish to rise to a fly which represents no known creature in the food chain. Or was it just aggression stimulated by a garish crimson flash? All mere speculation. As far as the rises under calm water conditions are concerned, there may be an explanation. It is possible that what was visible from underneath suggested a caterpillar. But that fly was stationary. Normal caterpillars do not zoom across the surface of a loch at high speed. Whatever the reason, I shall certainly be trying that Red Palmer again should the conditions seem propitious.

Angler (after landing his tenth—reading notice). "The man who wrote that sign couldn't have been using the right bait!"

Evolution

I am a great believer in chance. It has resulted in the creation of numerous highly successful patterns. An example which springs to mind is how Arthur Ransome's Elver-Fly came into being. As he relates in *Mainly About Fishing,* he was in a London hotel during the Second World War and, as he so delightfully expresses it, "...trying to forget London by thinking, naturally, about salmon ... Why on earth should the salmon, unable to eat in fresh water, be sometimes ready to take our flies?"

After observing some American soldiers in the hotel, chewing gum, he began to wonder if salmon taking flies in fresh water were not just going through some similar need to "chew". As a result of this observation Ransome went on to design his fly.

My adaptation of a Mayfly came about in a more roundabout way.

The second wife of my partner's ex-husband (modern relationships are just so complicated) came up with a very unusual present for my partner's son's new wife, a very beautiful Peruvian woman, who has found European temperatures, particularly in winter, more than a little trying.

The present: an Arctic Fox fur boa, which she discovered at a market in Spain, where she lives. This item of clothing was much in favour with ladies pursuing a particular profession in the early part of the last century. They (the boas, that is) today are less popular and are hence obtainable at very little expense. My eye was immediately caught by the texture and quality of the fur, and I asked the lady in question if she could look round for more on her visits to Spanish markets. Within a few weeks, I received a beautiful tail of Arctic Fox.

The next question was how to use this wonderful fur. On going through one of many fly-boxes accumulated in the course of a long life I suddenly noticed some Mayflies which I had only used once. They must be at least forty years old and were tied traditionally with fan-shaped wings which were designed, I sometimes now think, by someone who did not wish anglers to enjoy themselves. Such flies, when cast, spin like dervishes and twist the cast into terminal tangles. And even if a fish is actually caught, the wings are mostly then just a sticky mess and of no further use.

That's it, I thought. I took these flies and ripped out the wings, tied in the wonderful Arctic Fox fur, adding normal hackle in front of and behind the upright fur wing. I also cut off the underpart of the hackle so that the fly would then swim flat. The flies looked very appetizing. I found the time between tying and May very hard to wait through.

And then I found myself on the river bank with Mayflies rising all round me.

I put on that fly.

It was totally ignored!

Dog and Dogged Days

Why is it, I wonder, the Mayfly so seldom offers what tradition tells us it should? In a relatively long life, I can think of only rare occasions when conditions were such that even classical duffers would have been successful.

And again this year beside a river (the Lauterach in Bavaria) which I have now visited for nearly fifty years, initially held out tremendous promise. Apparently three days before my arrival there had been an explosive and massive hatch so that in spite of recent storms, one could imagine prospects to be, at the very least, promising.

The mill-owner was nevertheless not overly encouraging. He said that the fish could well already be full to bursting. I was not to be put off. At least not to begin with.

The weather could not have been more propitious: warm, humid, with excellent cloud cover. There were Spent on the water too to which occasional fish were rising. That was the moment when my spirits received an unexpected jolt. I suddenly discovered that I had only five Spents with me. I had left a box with at least fifty at home. I had also left my normal boots behind. I had chest-waders but with the likely temperatures I did not fancy putting them on. And so things continued. I drove along the river, looked at possible starting-points, but found it difficult to make up my mind where to begin.

In the end I went back to the mill and began fishing above the millstream. As I started, two children suddenly appeared, clearly intrigued by what this strange man was doing. He did not disappoint them. Immediately his cast became caught up a tree. Now only four Spents. A new cast had to be tied, which tried the patience of the children considerably. A fish rose to Spent number four. I struck too quickly. The children looked puzzled. I tried to explain, but I do not think they understood. I then hooked two fish, both of which came off. Then Spent number four was up a tree where it remained.

At this point the children drifted off. I doubt if either of them will wish to take up fly-fishing. It was one of those moments, too, when one's self-esteem dwindles rapidly. I then left that point to look for other, perhaps more promising spots along the river. I did not find any, and was almost at the point of giving up and returning home, so disgusted was I with my performance.

Before going any further, a slight digression. One of the many endlessly fascinating – and disturbing – aspects of fly-fishing for me has always been the confrontation with self, whether positive or negative. After all, if one has been lucky, one has had people in one's life who have helped to form one's performance and attitude. One is generally alone, and nevertheless constantly facing one's action. Whether good or bad. Again on this occasion I was confronted by a fisherman who was doing everything wrong. I was well aware of this, but how was I now to do something about it?

I then suddenly remembered fishing on another river two weeks before. Conditions had been even more difficult in that trout were rising, but not to anything we put in front of them. Again there were Spents and an occasional Mayfly. We moved from one spot to another along the river.

And then, for reasons I really don't understand, I decided to return to a place where fish had occasionally been taking, even if mostly underneath bushes where it was impossible to place a fly. I returned and decided to stay.

All at once fish began to move out into more open water. Within ten minutes I had hooked two fish, one of which I landed. It was only a very short period, but at least sticking it out had paid off.

Bearing that in mind, rather than cravenly giving up, I went back to the stretch above the millstream. I was now less nervous, but also resigned to facing what might happen.

There were occasional fish moving. As I was worried about losing my few remaining Spents, I put on a Mayfly. A trout came up, looked, and demonstratively turned away. I tied on a Spent. It worked. It worked. It worked. I was so relieved. Very much a matter of observation, careful and gentle presentation, and slower reactions.

The last fish was a case in point. I was standing near trees, beneath one of which was a deep backwater. I suddenly noticed a swirl in that space. It was a matter of just a few yards. I cast, waited. A fish rose, almost in slow motion, turned, went down. It was well-hooked and weighed a fraction under three pounds.

That day had certainly suddenly turned round.

A Sedge for all Seasons

As so often in life, a strange coincidence brought something to my attention. I was in the river, when I suddenly remembered I had to make a telephone call. Luckily there was a telephone booth only a short distance from where I was. I struggled up the bank and entered the booth in my chest waders. It was a very hot day so that I made a point of not talking too long. As I put down the receiver I suddenly sensed something. On looking up I saw a stationary car and four pairs of eyes concentrated on my overheated person. As soon as those in the car realized I had seen them, they left the scene at great speed. A creature from outer space?

I was about to open the door when I noticed something on the window outside. A sedge. Nothing very unusual about that. What however was very intriguing was that the fly was seen from underneath. Which, after all, is how fish will see, or register, such insects.

What suddenly struck me was that the body of the sedge was flush with the surface of the pane.

And that gave me an idea.

I had noticed that certain patterns of sedge, particularly those with feather wings, had a tendency to float unnaturally, the wings going down, rather than up.

The idea could not have been simpler: why not cut off the hackles underneath? It worked. Wonderfully. The tying could not have been easier. First, body material, then fur wing. To make sure the wing remains firm I add glue. An upward angle can be achieved by placing the fur against the body. I then used two or three hackles, cut from underneath. The colour, both of wings and body, can be varied according to what one expects to be hatching. If intended for night fishing, the fly can be given white wings which certainly increases visibility in the dark. It does not seem to put the fish off. I'm not fussy about the kind of fur: fox, deer, beaver.

This tying has caught me fish in many many rivers and lakes. I would not suggest it is original, but it couldn't be simpler to tie – and it *does* catch fish.

It has also had other consequences, as the following little anecdote may indicate. Some years ago, I was staying beside Lough Erne in August – not the best of fishing months. One afternoon I went off in the boat and finished up in a small bay. It was warm, cloudy, not a breath of wind. Suddenly some hundreds of yards away I noticed a disturbance on the surface. On this lough fish sometimes, particularly during the Mayfly, will travel distances, feeding all the time. I cast out in the direction the fish was taking, and waited. The fly suddenly disappeared violently. A beautiful brown trout, well over three pounds. That was fine. What was not so wonderful was that while playing that fish, I somehow twisted my body, and spent the next three days in agony as I had done something to my back. On the other hand, it is so wonderful when things work out…

Which reminds me of another good trout which rose to a Daddy in September on the same lough. Again I saw the fish approaching, made my preparations, cast. The fish was on. At that moment, an oar slipped overboard, I slipped on something, fell over the seat and finished up sitting in my own landing net. The fish meanwhile had left for quieter waters!

And in connection with that particular tying, perhaps an extract from a letter sent me by a friend:

Dear Jo,

I thought I would drop you a line to let you know that your sedges worked very well for me on lough Carra when I was there a month ago.

I have to confess that I didn't catch many decent-sized fish but the best I caught and the big one that got away were both on your sedge. The one I got was 3 ¾ lb and I got it by casting into the edge of the reeds and letting it sit there. The fish took with a little quiet confident rise and was on. I must admit I thought it was a bit of a fluke and so didn't try it again as much as I should. Then on my last evening I was just fooling about after catching a few small ones and I did the same again. He jumped and I saw he was very large. He made for the reeds and I tried to stop him. The cast broke halfway up. I realized I had had a knotted and frayed cast which I had been too lazy to change at the end of the trip. So aggravating not to have fished like that more, instead of thinking the first occasion was a fluke.

Best wishes

Nick

Contemplative Man (*in punt*). "I don't so much care about the sport, it's the delicious repose I enjoy s

Logic and a Split Decision

The Managing Director
House of Hardy
Alnwick   25 October 2009

Dear Sir,

May I draw to your attention a matter which has caused me much embarrassment, and friends to whom it has been related, endless amusement.

While on a fishing holiday recently, the top section of a rod from your company inexplicably broke. I wrote to you and was advised that I should return the section in question. This I did.

As a result of my letter, I then received another top section of this rod, for which many thanks.

However, this still leaves me with a problem.

When I returned the broken section, I assumed – from past experience with other manufacturers – that I would receive a complete new rod. As a consequence, I put the other sections into the dustbin. With the result that I now have a perfect new top section to a rod for which I now have no use, since I no longer have the other parts.

Perhaps you would be good enough to suggest how this unfortunate situation can be remedied.

Yours faithfully

(Eventually I was sent the other parts at a price which was fair – if still painful)

DRY-FLY ENTOMOLOGY. — (Scene — *The banks of a Hampshire stream in the graylin season*). *Angler* (*the rise having abruptly ceased*). "I think they're taking a *siesta*, Thompson *Keeper*. "I dessay they are, sir, but any other fly with a touch o' red in it would do as well."

A Conn-undrum

This is a mystery which goes back at least forty years. I wonder if it will ever be resolved. Probably not. Human sloth is something which, if anything, tends to intensify with time.

Several quite extraordinary days. Yet things could not have started more inauspiciously. I remember as if it was yesterday. There was a stiff easterly wind blowing across Lough Conn. The sun burned down. September. Conditions could hardly have been worse. We stopped the car and discussed what we would do.

In the end we decided to stay. What seemed the point of travelling to other venues if the weather was likely to remain as it was where we were?

At least we knew we were in good hands. As boatmen we had Pedraig Kelly and his redoubtable father, so we knew that even if no fish were rising we'd be regaled with stories from the moment we entered the boat. It is now such a long time ago that I cannot remember any of what was related except for the answer to a question. I once asked Pedraig's father what he thought about potheen. His answer: "Well, we give it to the animals when they're sick."

As expected, conditions were tough. No fish showed. At least to start with. We fished the usual way, three wet flies. Cast after cast after cast. On looking round in the direction of other boats, we had the impression that others were not faring any better.

I can't now remember who first noticed what was to be our deliverance: the appearance above the water, occasionally on the water, of strange black flies. Initially they looked like bluebottles. But bluebottles do not normally land or bounce on water. Additionally, these flies had a dark green sheen across their backs. To this day, I've not been able to determine what these creatures were. I would assume they came off the land, but whatever they were, they provided us with inspiration. We noticed that fish were moving to these flies. This was surprising, considering the conditions, and the fact that they were not in clouds, but just individual insects moving across the lough.

The next question: What did we have which would satisfactorily represent these creatures? A very simple solution presented itself. A Black and Peacock Spider. The fact that our patterns did not have a green sheen on their backs did not seem to upset the trout. And on the top dropper.

We did not catch large numbers although we did catch large fish. Up to four pounds, which is big by Lough Conn standards.

The other anglers were very surprised at our success and cross-examined or rather, wanted to cross-examine us. Pedraig's father was a very competitive person, and had given us strict instructions as to how we were to behave.

As we came into the bay, he bellowed – "NO, NO, NO! Let them find out for themselves."

I regret to say that we remained very non-committal.

One little after-note. That fly with something gleaming green on the back has sometimes in the meanwhile saved difficult days on lakes.

"NOT PROVEN."—*Presbyterian Minister*. "Don't you know it's wicked to catch fish on the Sawbath?!"
Small Boy (not having had a rise all the morning). "Wha's catchin' fesh?!"

An Unusual Experience

Lough Erne is perfect for those who enjoy self-imposed suffering. The trout are wild, wily, and at most times of the year have no need to rise anywhere near the surface in search of food. Mayfly time is traditionally when even such fish can be tempted, if conditions should be right. Unfortunately May in Northern Ireland is an extremely unpredictable month as far as weather is concerned. The only thing one can assert with any certainty is that one will have weather. In fact I can remember one day in that month when all seasons were represented and I arrived at the lough in a snow-storm. There was a mad rise of Mayflies until the moment I reached the bay where fish had been moving.

And that is Lough Erne in a nutshell. It is dour, unpredictable, is not for those who are not prepared to try, and try, and try again.

Even when conditions seem ideal – at least to the angler – that is no guarantee that Lough Erne trout will appreciate this and start rising.

Nevertheless this lough holds trout of size and majesty. And that is what draws anglers back year after year. For those who can only stay for period of days, this also makes the likelihood of catching the fish of a lifetime distinctly remote. But it can happen. As I will relate.

Some years ago I had almost given up. Weather conditions had been dire. Cold, windy, wintry. One Saturday afternoon I decided I would watch tennis. The French Open. At some stage I suddenly glanced through the window. The trees were no longer moving. I got up and went outside. A sudden change. It was warm, muggy, with total cloud cover. Tennis was forgotten. I had a sudden feeling.

I still don't know why I drove to a particular bay to the right of Eagle Point. That area is notable for pike, though trout are sometimes caught off islands and along some shores. Halfway up I stopped the boat and let it drift. Never have I seen such a concentrated rise to Spents. As far as the eye could discern, fish were moving. Big fish.

One problem for the occasional angler on a lough like Erne is that one has little chance of getting into some kind of rhythm. If, after hours of casting, a fish suddenly rises to the fly, there is an almost inevitable tendency to snatch. This happened with my first fish. The cast broke. In the event this was fortuitous as I then tied on stronger nylon.

Fish rising to Spent often move at great speed. I registered movement at least a hundred yards away. The fish approached rising regularly, and fast. I left a Spent in his path. The trout took with a rush and was on. There was no holding this fish. I have never, in over forty years, experienced such strength. This fish actually, at one stage, towed the boat. The struggle went on for nearly forty minutes, although I held hard. Finally the pressure eased.

And then, horror of horrors, I discovered that in my haste to get out, I had omitted to put a net in the boat. I looked round desperately. There had been another boat not far from me. It was still there. I waved and shouted. Those in that boat suddenly realized there was a problem and came over, so that I was after all permitted to land that fish. It weighed exactly five pounds, not large by Lough Erne standards. It was bright silver and looked more like a grilse than a trout. A local angler later suggested that it may possibly have been a slob trout which had come into the lough from the estuary.

So, for once, things had worked out.

On that same afternoon, another angler caught four trout between two and four pounds, before hooking a fish he estimated at ten, which he lost at the net. The net wasn't big enough!

Lunatic (suddenly popping his head over wall). "What are you doing there?" *Brown.* "Fishing." *Lunatic.* "Caught anything?" *Brown.* "No." *Lunatic.* "How long have you been there?" *Brown.* "Six hours." *Lunatic.* "Come inside!"

Fun and Failure

Somehow one often remembers mishaps more clearly than occasions when everything goes right. I am sure that any fisherman will still see with total clarity fish which, for some reason or other, have not stayed on. They remain before the mind's eye, held there for ever, in animated suspension.

Sometimes it seems as if fate is definitely not on one's side. This year has so far been accompanied by a whole series of unhappy developments.

For example, I had been so looking forward to returning to the Hebrides in May. I did return to the Hebrides. I arrived in a force nine gale. The outside temperature was between five and seven degrees centigrade. The rain against one's face struck like icy needles. After reading the weather forecast for the coming week, I decided to leave after only two days.

And so things have continued. The Mayfly was a perfect follow-up. I had planned to go down to Bavaria to a stream I have fished for decades. The weather this year has been very strange, so I phoned in advance to ask how things were going. I was told I would be too early, so postponed. When I next telephoned, it was to be informed that the Mayfly had actually started properly the weekend I had wished to travel. I was prevented from going down the weekend after, so that was that.

On another river, I went to a section I did not know well, and waited, waited, and waited. Nothing happened, so I went home. When I phoned a friend the next day he told me that the hatch started exactly ten minutes after I had gone. He then went on to relate, in great detail, the size and number of fish he had caught. When I made arrangements to go again, my visit coincided with a sudden and violent storm which turned the river into a raging torrent within a very short space of time.

This reminded me of a very strange week in Ireland many years ago, on a tributary of the River Moy, which then held some very good brown trout. Again at Mayfly time. For one reason or another I hardly managed to get, or stay, in contact with fish all week. This went on until the last day when things changed and I remained firmly attached to all the fish that rose.

This year's woes have continued. On the Ahr, a most beautiful stream near the Belgian border, I happened to be there at a moment which coincided with a slightly unusual hatch of Mayfly. In mid-July. I was briefly attached to a very large brown trout, which I saw as it went down. I then, rather late, discovered that the sharp end of my hook was missing. I say "rather late" because this was after not connecting with several fish which rose to the fly.

But so things continued. After inexplicably not catching several more fish, I suddenly discovered that the cast had wrapped round the hook and was knotted at the barb. I gave up.

And one final episode to round off a season of discontent. Another visit to the Hebrides. In the course of six hard days on hard seats in hard weather, I landed one two-pound brownie. I occasionally encountered other creatures which I did not see because they inexplicably came off. On the last day, almost immediately, I hooked a three-pound trout which jumped and dashed, before departing, for the nearest horizon. Three days of thundery weather had a further dampening effect on both grilse and sea trout.

But there were other curious happenings. Twice on the same day I thought I was finally firmly and excitingly attached to something huge. In both cases it turned out that relatively small trout had somehow caught the fly where no fly had any business to be, nevertheless contributing to the illusion that my run of bad luck was about to end. It wasn't, and didn't.

In the meanwhile I am beginning to find this season something of a joke. But perhaps one last little anecdote. I occasionally handed the rod over to our wonderful boatman. On one of such occasions, on his third or fourth cast, he foul-hooked a beautiful and big brownie which, of course, stayed on.

EGOMANIA.—(Scene—*The Bar Parlour of the "Little Peddlington Arms" during a shower.*) *Little dlingtonian (handing newspaper to stranger from London).* " Have you seen that account of our fishing npetition in the *Little Peddlington Gazette*, sir ? " " No, I'm afraid I've not ! " ' It's a *very* eresting article, sir. It mentions my name several times ! "

Letter to a Friend

7 December 2005

Dear Nick,

I have in front of me a book entitled *Grumpy Old Men.* Subtitle: *A Manual for the British Malcontent.* And I think that just about sums up Yours Truly and his present state.

You've very kindly let me have two books to read and I am proving intransigently unreceptive and ungrateful – for which I apologise sincerely. Most sincerely.

I hope you will bear with me if I try to get down to what it is that has provoked an irk. I think, in essence, it's the attempt to make something profound, something philosophical, something almost religious about a hobby. And a certain holier than thou attitude. For example, the grotesque situation in one chapter when the fourteen-year-old son goes into a near catatonic fit when he sees a fish being bashed on the head. As if catch-and-release is something higher, gentler, and eminently more praiseworthy than catching fish for the frying-pan.

The chapter on England and the raising of coarse fishermen well above the status of fly-fishermen solely because they catch but don't kill just has more hackles rise. It reminds me of reports of some American rivers in which trout have been caught so often that their jaws are just jagged and pitted pieces of decrepit mortality.

There's something in me which rebels against the raising of a possibly indefensible activity to the level of the morally uplifting. If asked, I would actually find it very difficult to justify what I do when on the wrong end of a fishing rod. Not that there is a right end! But catching fish just to release them in essence brings to my attention most painfully just what it is I am doing when out angling.

In one sense my gripes are definitely open to challenge, in that for many years fishing offered me the only means of getting away – if only briefly – from a dire domestic tangle. Fishing has always been a means

34

of getting away from things. That I refuse to be upset by what I do is certainly something that I might – indeed occasionally do – think about.

I fear too I tend to react allergically to the kind of overspeak in certain sections. (p.107)

"When I see fish coming through the water, they seem as self-contained and sovereign as beings from another planet ... "

From further down:

"Trout are like dreams hovering in the illusive unconscious. In capturing one, if ever so briefly, before release (here we go again!) *there is that sense of revelation occurring when one awakens in the night, snatching a dream from the dark portals of sleep."*

This passage actually reminds me of my first poem, written in the dark portals of puberty, which ran as follows:

"I dropped my fly right over his nose,

And what was my joy when from the bottom he rose,

And so I deceived the fish of my dream:

That pink-spotted beauty, the king of the stream."

Completely in character, as the rest of this deathless poem reveals, that was one king that bit the dust. And I am deliberately mixing my metaphors here. At the age of 15 I had never caught anything over half a pound. So it was either wishful thinking or poetic licence. In any case, further proof that bad writing will result when the thinking behind it is dishonest.

I do hope you won't think me both insensitive and ungrateful. I personally feel a great debt of gratitude, because through your lending me those books, you have forced me to do some quite serious thinking.

For that, too, very sincere thanks.

CONSCIENTIOUS FLATTERY.—*Boatman.* " I canna mind a finer fesh for its size!"

Ego-denting

A few years ago I was invited to fish a small river on the edge of the Black Forest in Germany, a stretch which in the past had given me some excellent sport. On the day in question, although conditions were good, I came across few trout – at least in the lower section of the river. I assumed this was a result of serious predation by cormorants, although I actually didn't see any that day. This stretch of the river was rarely fished and the trout had always been both numerous and willing. On previous visits I had always caught a fair number of good-sized trout, but I was becoming a little worried that I might return home empty-handed.

There was one section of the river which I had always avoided, as it included the extensive and ruined premises of a derelict factory; not exactly attractive surroundings for angling. However I was still fishless and this section was my last hope.

As I walked along the road I looked down into the river with no great expectations. To my amazement, I discerned fish rising near (and under) a bridge. I stopped and looked more carefully. I then slipped down the bank and into the water. The flow of water against my back was fairly strong and I was forced to cast downstream. This meant waiting longer than usual before striking. Just as I started I noticed an elderly man had walked onto the bridge and was staring intently at what I was doing. I proceeded to catch four or five trout, all of a good size. Feeling rather pleased with myself, I clambered up the bank again and found myself facing the elderly man.

I asked him if he came to the bridge regularly. "Oh yes", he said. "Every day I come here with my grandson to feed the fish. They are very tame." "Oh!" was all I could manage before walking away quickly.

Letter to *Fly-Fishing and Fly-Tying*

A Moment in Time

Life can be so strange. As a result of serious illness in the family, it became almost impossible for me to think of going fishing. Or, for that matter, even want to fish.

And then something quite unexpected happened. I was told, in no uncertain terms, that I was to take myself off and go fishing. I obeyed.

The beginning of June, the possibility of Mayfly. There is one stretch of river which docs have big hatches. I thought I might, for once, be fortunate. I arrived. The river was up slightly, very fast-flowing, and had a brownish tinge. I actually saw one or two Mayflies, but no surface activity whatsoever. I stayed for a while and then decided to go to an upper stretch where there are always fly on the water and the trout are good risers, even if I had never experienced any serious response to the occasional Mayflies which rested on the surface.

There is one pool, just above the millstream, where good fish may be encountered. At this point the river is more of a brook and rarely more than two or three yards wide.

Some years ago, while fishing with a friend, I noticed an insect on his pullover – a willow-fly. I was rather taken by its appearance and tied up a pattern I hoped would work: thin tail (fur) and above it two small grizzle hackles, cut off underneath so that the fly would float directly in the surface.

There were rises in the middle section. With each of the first five casts I was into fish, one of which came off. However, within the first few minutes, to rise and hook every fish is very unusual, but highly gratifying, particularly since one of those fish was just under one and a half pounds, which is above average for that particular stretch.

Just before the water is diverted to the left into the millstream, there is both a metal gate which can be raised or lowered to control the level of flow and, directly behind it, a grating with metal bars going into the water. Presumably to prevent debris passing down the millstream.

For a long time I had been thinking about that little area just above and below the gate. I had a strong suspicion that really big fish could be encountered there. All at once I noticed movement just in front of where the grating entered the water. I had a sudden thought. Although there is normally no real rise to Mayfly, perhaps it might be worth a try. At least any fish would notice a fly of that size. Some years ago, I tied a whole series of Mayflies using cul de canard. I don't know why, but I had never actually cast one to a fish. Before going any further, a little aside. Reaching that rise involved a very tricky cast, letting out line, with the danger of the fly getting caught. I was suddenly reminded of a statement by G.E.M. Skues. He mentions the strange phenomenon of fishermen spending huge amounts of money on angling equipment, but then not casting into a space surrounded by hazards, for fear of losing a fly worth pennies! Thus, possibly, missing the opportunity of catching the fish of a lifetime. However I will not deny that I did entertain initial concern that the fly might go missing!

I think I shall never forget watching that Mayfly, drifting gently down the pool, seductively emitting yellowy green gleams. The fly reached that crucial area between gate and grating. A rise. The fish was on and, to my great relief, surged upstream. I held hard. Had it gone through the grating, there's no way I could have avoided a break.

Then I suddenly caught sight of this fish. I could not believe it. A huge brown trout. I do not think I have ever, in more than sixty years of fishing, seen such a beautiful fish, so perfectly proportioned. In the clear water I could perceive all the amazing colours and markings. It was like the portrait of a trout.

As so often in small waters, this fish did not fight violently, just pulled and pulled and pulled. And then it was in the net. It must have weighed between four and five pounds. Somehow I could not permit myself to take it out of its true element, and returned it, holding on until it righted itself and swam slowly away. I had absolutely no regrets. Only a never-ending sense of wonderment that nothing had gone wrong. I even remembered that shortly before, I had been in contact with a branch, and the cast had broken at a knot which I had been too lazy to deal with!

DREADFUL SITUATION!

Party in Waders (on the shallower side, with nice trout on).
" Now then, you idiot, bring me the net, can't you, or he'll
be off in a second !"

Itching to Fish

Mark Bowler's delightful article on the rivers near the Gave d'Oloron (*France's secret corner*, November 2008) struck a nostalgic nerve. I was reminded of a trip to that very area nearly fifty years ago after my brother discovered a tempting announcement in The Times of the angling delights to be discovered in this, for us, unknown region. Tantalising references to salmon and trout in the area caused us to book in at a chateau whose address was revealed in the same announcement.

The chateau in question was run by an elderly Englishwoman who told us several times a day that she had been born in St. Petersburg. The furniture in the house was notable not only for its antiquity, but also its fragility. After several embarrassing breakages we took to sitting down slowly. And very gingerly.

We had the freedom of the countryside. This meant that we travelled to many waters, all seemingly pristine, and equally lacking in the one reason for visiting: fish.

The lack of piscatorials was well balanced by the presence in our beds, and also on our persons, of insects noted for their hopping and biting propensities. Indeed, on rising each morning, we stepped first into our makeshift flea-trap – a bath of cold water. There we stood waiting for the sated horrors to drop off.

In the course of that itchy week we ran up a painful total. It became increasingly embarrassing as we continued to return from lengthy fishing expeditions with very little to show for all our hard work.

On the day of our departure, our hostess asked – no doubt so she could make an entry in the game book – what the sum total of our catches was. Somewhat sheepishly one of us made the following admission: "48 fleas and one one-eyed trout." This statement was greeted with raucous laughter.

Letter to *"Fly-Fishing And Fly-Tying"*, January 2009

The End of the Day

Some months ago I was approached in a round-about way and asked if I would be prepared to contribute to a *Where to Fish* in Germany. Before giving a categorical answer, I thought it might be wise to consult the editor of one of the two main German fly-fishing magazines. His response, to put it mildly, surprised me. "Are you mad? Or have you taken a course in mendacity?" followed by a raucous laugh. He then went on to confirm at national level what I have experienced on a river which I have been fishing for some thirty years. Pollution, inadvertent or deliberate damming; alteration of river courses; the making accessible to city dwellers of small waters and lakes, and now, terminally, the protection of cormorants and mergansers, have reduced fish-stocks and in some cases almost eliminated a whole species: grayling.

When first thinking about writing such an article, I suddenly began to wonder if the placing of the cormorant on the protected list was not perhaps a brilliant tactical move on the part of the Greens and animal rights lobby to put an end to fishing, not by banning the sport but by eliminating the fish. In many parts of Germany and Switzerland this has happened.

For example, I recently saw a film about one lake and river in Switzerland which have an annual visitation of cormorants now running into thousands. One was shown Range Rovers being driven up and down a stretch of river where grayling spawn. Vehicles have to be kept moving constantly from dawn to dusk to prevent elimination of remaining stocks. On the river I fished for many years, numbers of grayling which over a stretch of some eleven kilometres ran into thousands, have been reduced to almost nil over a period of only four years. In fact until recently, I cannot remember ever having seen any cormorants at all. Now each autumn many hundreds arrive, to stay until March. A colony of about seventy has established itself near the reservoir above our water. The effect on trout stocks has also been devastating.

All this on a stretch of river which until six or seven years ago was one of the best in Europe. Trout up to ten and eleven pounds have been caught and any number between three and six. One local poacher was found on the bank. Dead. Beside him a great trout of nine pounds. What a way to go!

Looking back, one can reconstruct the manner in which decline set in. Firstly caravan sites at two places beside the river. These resulted in poaching and disturbance. Later, cycle paths were put in along the river, right through a bird sanctuary. In recent years one has had to face the comments and jeers of canoeists as they passed on in flotillas, ripping up weed on their way.

There was one area right in front of the high dam where one could nearly always be certain of finding fish, whatever the height of the water. An underwater wall kept out pike, and provided standing-room right across the river. This was an area in which specimen fish could be, and frequently were, encountered. The dam wall has been taken down and renewed in the past couple of years. The habitat has changed completely, and now there are only one or two large cannibal trout competing for territory with pike.

The final blow has come with the arrival and establishment of cormorants. Permission has been given for some culling. Interestingly enough, on smaller rivers, cormorants have been kept away by stretching cord across and above the surface, thus preventing the birds from landing.

Since protecting cormorants was a political decision, one might have assumed that legal redress might be an avenue worth pursuing. Again quite wrong. The increase in numbers of natural species is a "natural phenomenon" and hence human law may not be applied. An incredibly vicious circle. Sadly, as things now stand, it seems unlikely that the situation can ever improve. With the result that a fishery which has been in the hands of responsible anglers for over a hundred years and with such a healthy head of resident fish that stocking was never necessary is now under terminal threat.

Perhaps, to finish, a short description of some hours spent on the river at the end of the season in 1978.

What a bagful of surprises, some pleasant, some not so pleasant. The

German army had taken possession – for the purpose of some military exercise, of surrounding roads, fields and much of the air. I was on the point of entering the river and approaching a weedbed where some very big fish tend to rest late in the season. Suddenly a helicopter appeared over the top of the dam like a huge grasshopper and remained stationary above where I had intended to start. The calm surface of the water was broken as if a huge mirror had shattered. The helicopter remained suspended there for about five minutes. No fish moved at that spot for the rest of the day.

Down to my favourite part of the river: At first fast-flowing but not deep, followed by shallows before widening. The current flows in narrow channels along both banks, leaving a calmer deeper section in the middle filled with weed. In the spaces between the weed big fish will be found at this time of the year. These are spawning fish which have come upriver but which cannot go any further, since the dam is impassable. Trees, bushes and rushes provide a rich and varied supply of insects.

I moved out into the weed to where I had seen a fish move. I cast. A boil. The fish roared off. It was half-way round me before I could move. The line threw up spray as the fish turned, fortunately moving upstream, jagging violently, desperately trying to return into the weeds. I held hard. The fish turned downstream, and I just had to follow. It was the strongest fish I had ever encountered on that river. A real Eder trout, perfectly proportioned. These fish have a greeny tinge and always seem to be in superb condition. Since I had seen the fish come out of the water, even held it at rod's length in the current ahead of me, I could see that it was at least three pounds. Do what I could, it would not come out of the current. Finally it seemed played out. It hung motionless, head and tail showing when the hook came away. For once I had no reason the reproach myself. Hemingway would have said it was a "brave" fish. It deserved to get away.

Just perhaps one other outstanding memory, towards the end of the good times. I had met up with a friend from the club. We sat on a bench beside the river at a point and time of year when weed ran down in long strips. We knew we would have to wait until dusk. Then we would step into the water, and try to place our flies so that they would float down between the lines of weed. I slipped in after my friend. He went down, I moved upriver. It was one of those evenings, soft, warm, with sedges beginning to move. And not only sedges. I noticed a movement in the water just ahead of me. I cast. I was fortunate the fly landed just where it should. I sensed movement, tightened.

It was necessary to hold hard. Even so, the fish managed to get into the weed. I increased pressure but did not strain. Slowly, ever so slowly, I gained control. I knew I was into something big. Slowly, slowly, slowly, the trout emerged from the weed. Interestingly, big fish sometimes did not fight as hard at night as during the day. As in this instance. A 4 lb brown trout in perfect condition. I took it over to the bank, got out of the water, and sat there, waiting for my friend to return.

It was one of those wonderful moments, of which there had been so many, which now will never return.

Bavaria's Dr Duncan

Many decades ago there was excellent trout fishing to be had in many parts of Germany: notably in Bavaria and Baden Württemberg. Some Englishmen's records can still be read: Harry Plunket Greene's description of Black Forest trout being perhaps the most delightful and entertaining. There we learn of trout by the bucketful and even of one which, though bloated with sausage, was unable to resist a "fat March Brown".

I have been living in Germany for many years now and have explored some of the areas in which Plunket Greene had such happy times. Today, as everywhere in Europe, things are not what they once were. Nowhere is this perhaps as striking as in the part of Bavaria known as Franconian Switzerland which lies roughly between Bayreuth and Nürnberg. it is limestone country, undulating, intersected by narrow river valleys which are overlooked by pine, oak and beech forests on the steep slopes. In summer the upper reaches of most of the crystal clear streams become a mess of tents and tourists, and the rivers are churned up by canoeists. Some of these rivers, such as the Wiesent, Pegnitz and Lauterach, used to hold good stocks of large trout and grayling.

Before the last war, a number of enterprising Englishmen came over to Germany every year to enjoy sport which today most of us dream of but rarely experience. On trips to this part of the country, I have constantly heard tales of one fisherman in particularly, a man who fished the Bavarian rivers for much of his life and who returned to the Wiesent in his eighties, a sick man: so sick that he had to be taken to a hospital in Forchheim, where he died.

There seemed to be uncertainty about his nationality and profession – probably to be ascribed to the curious inaccuracy of human memory. Some people said Dr Duncan was Irish, some that he was English. Some said he was a scientist, others that he was a minister in the British government. All agreed, however, that he was a great fisherman.

Before his arrival on the scene, the local method of fly-fishing on the river Lauterach consisted in hurling March Browns and Alexandras mounted on size eight hooks across the river and working these downstream. The trout of those days, not having been brought up on Halford, eagerly snapped up these unnatural baits. Dr Duncan soon did something about that. He taught the local lads the art of the dry fly and soon it was only the older generation who persisted in using the large and clumsy flies which had done such good service until then. To us, of course, Dr Duncan would seem to be a perfect example of the old school. Before fishing he would first go to the bridge, there to watch for and catch whatever fly were hatching. If he did not have the appropriate artificials – which can seldom have happened – he would quickly tie some. Local farms were regularly inspected. Whenever he saw a suitable cockerel, he would buy it, telling the surprised farmer not to kill the bird until the feathers were just right.

Dr Duncan, whose German was perfect, was a splendid narrator of tall tales, although it is mostly stories about him which one hears today. Apparently, if a willing person could be found, he would cast a fly from the bridge into the outstretched hand of someone standing on the bank. Some of his conversations with a local inn-keeper became a kind of ritual. For example, he would say on leaving: "Hans, I am now going out to the river. I shall proceed along the bank, ignoring the small fish until I see a trout worthy of my skill. That fish I shall catch." An hour or so later, Dr Duncan would return. On being asked what success he had had, the answer was, invariably: "Oh, nothing but tiddlers!"

He must have been a brilliant fly-tyer. One of his favourite creations went by the appropriate name of "Duncan's Indecent". Whenever he opened the box containing these flies, he would keep one hand over it – as he would explain – to prevent the naturals from being exposed to temptation. He also maintained that the fly had to be kept moving fast along the surface of the water or it would be sunk by a swarm of buzzing suitors.

His diminutive figure, humping a huge fishing basket or, more often sitting on it, must have been a familiar sight along the banks of Bavarian rivers decades ago. He used to let younger friends go on ahead while he would sit and wait for a good trout to show. Such excellent chalk-stream tactics were generally rewarded with the success they deserved. Dr Duncan was certainly an eccentric. He seldom arrived with less than nine pieces of baggage, at least eight of these containing angling equipment. Although he was good at so many things, driving was not to be numbered among them. One summer in the twenties he arrived at his favourite hotel in one of those enormously impressive automobiles which seemed to consist almost entirely of bonnet. After several unsuccessful attempts to take this machine into the car park, through a very narrow entrance, he finally asked the hotel-keeper to do it for him – which he was no doubt very glad to do. After this, the car was always driven by the hotel-keeper whenever Dr Duncan came to the Lauterach. This too was not without consequence. On one occasion they went to Amberg, a small neighbouring town, to meet some friends of Dr Duncan. The large motor-car with its foreign number plate caused a minor sensation. Dr Duncan went off to do some shopping before his friends arrived, leaving Hans sitting at the wheel of the open car which was parked on the wrong side of the main street. Some students gathered round and discussed the car, and where it was parked, at some length; all of them assuming that Hans, who was dressed in Bavarian costume (including leather trousers) was English – an impression he strengthened by picking up an English newspaper which he pretended to read. One of the students finally plucked up courage and told the driver, in halting English, that parking was forbidden there. Hans, quickly mustering two of the few English words he knew, answered: "Thank you!" and drove to the other side. The students also crossed to road with the obvious intention of continuing such a promising conversation. At this moment one of Hans' friends passed and shouted in German: "That's a splendid motor-car you have there, Hans!" The students slunk away in great discomfiture.

At that time there were only two radio sets in the whole village. Dr Duncan, who was a wealthy man, kept racehorses. He used to give the owner of one of the radio sets the equivalent of a pound so that he could hear the racing results. Reception was not very good, so Dr Duncan gave the owner of the other radio a pound as well: on condition that he did not ever use the set, except to hear the racing news!

One could go on endlessly telling stories of this remarkable man. If sport may be said to improve international relations – nowadays a somewhat dubious assertion – then Dr Duncan certainly made his contribution. Happiness was a quality seemingly possessed by many of those who fished in earlier times and who wrote about their hobby. Plunket Greene says of his own fishing water: "… for if ever there was a happy river in this world it was the little Hampshire Bourne." I don't know if Dr Duncan ever published anything. Probably not. Most of the great fishermen have been modest men. Nevertheless, it is pleasing to discover that Dr Duncan is not forgotten today, and that stories about him continue to be told which reflect in quiet places positive aspects of a sport he loved.

Kingsmill Moore and Ballynahinch

I am well aware that there is no obvious connection between the two names mentioned in the title of this piece. However there is a very personal connection which I will come to later.

Through a strange series of coincidences I was privileged to have some contact with Kingsmill Moore, met him twice and corresponded with him for a short period of time before the second edition of his wonderful book *A Man May Fish* appeared. Sadly he did not live to see this, as he died shortly before the book was published.

I've just been glancing through the letters he wrote to me at this period. Again I am struck by the force of character which emerges from every word he writes. He was already in his early eighties, but his mind and wit were as sharp as they had obviously always been.

Two examples:

"...I have just finished the chapter on Alec and Delphi and am sending it to be typed. I made a rough draft and found it full of clichés so, mindful of your eye, I took them out. The result looked so arid that I have just put most of them back!"

"I think you, in common with most modern critics, are too hard on the cliché. It is a word of variable and uncertain meaning, often used as a general word of abuse for something the critic particularly detests. I defend the cliché. If we use common words because they are the right words why not use common phrases because they are thought phrases. Of course even an apt phrase may become so threadbare from over-use that it loses its impact. But you condemn many expressions which to me are still full of meaning."

There was also nothing wrong with his eyesight. I took the liberty of sending him some flies I had had tied – at the time I still hadn't started fly-tying myself. His comments indicate just how sharp his eyes still were:

"*Claret Bumble: on the whole this is well tied. The jay front hackle should be more prominent.*

Blue Bumble: much too blue. Additionally my book is very specific that a black hackle should be wound with the blue which tones it down.

Golden Olive Bumble: This should have a jay hackle in front. Your specimen has a grey partridge hackle (which may at one time have been dyed blue, then faded)."

Kingsmill Moore was also a wonderful conversationalist and raconteur. By a strange coincidence, just before we met for the first time, I had attended a trial, also for the first time. I became so fascinated by the proceedings that I stayed for nearly ten days, unfortunately not being able to remain until final judgment was made. What had concerned me in the course of my attendance was that had I been a member of the jury, I do not know how I would have decided. Since Kingsmill Moore had been a very eminent professional lawyer, I took the liberty of asking him how he came to make up his mind. I was given an answer which took me totally by surprise:

"*At some stage in every trial, I suddenly have an inkling, a feeling. I respond to that.*"

I was astounded because this was not the kind of answer I would have expected from a professional who had gone through all the normal processes of legal and deductive thought. However, in retrospect, I think I can now understand how this must have come about. If one listens to two sides in a legal confrontation, the arguments are presented so cogently and appear to make such sense that it must often be extremely difficult for a judge, in summing up, to indicate to the jury how things really stand. That Kingsmill Moore gave me such an honest and direct answer to my question is for me just one more indication of what a rare and wonderful personality he was. His book *A Man May Fish* breathes that humanity and generosity on every page.

But what, one may ask, has all this to do with personal reminiscences of Ballynahinch? The answer is very simple. Everything. It was through something I read in Kingsmill Moore's book which gave me some of the most wonderful and successful sea trout fishing I have ever experienced. Even if now, sadly, a thing of the past. The introduction of a salmon farm in the estuary reduced catches of sea trout from 3000 in a normal year, to just 80. I stopped going.

But back to the beginning. On the first visit we were shown round by the head ghillie, a delightful and most helpful fisherman, Michael. I remember one incident as if it was yesterday. Largely because of the enormous embarrassment it caused me. At the beginning we mostly fished nights, with occasional forays to specific places. One of these was the area just above Beat One where the lough flowed in. This was a spot where sea trout were nearly always to be found.

As indeed on this occasion. There were rings and swirls. I thought I would try with a dry fly. I did try with a dry fly. That fly provoked savage rises. In not one case did I connect with what was rising, although I am sure some of those fish were very large indeed. The Ballynahinch did produce very big sea trout. At one stage I turned round. Michael, very discreetly, had withdrawn. Something I myself did shortly after.

That was one aspect – to which I will return. There was also night fishing, which could be very good indeed. There too we were given wonderful advice by some Northern Irish fishermen who returned year after year. They showed us the best and most likely lies. There our previous experience stood us in good stead.

There was also one incident in connection with the Northern Irish fishermen which we found we too could laugh about. Eventually. After one very successful visit, the group returned home and spread the catch out on the lawn so that a photograph could be made. A count was made, which resulted in great surprise. There seemed to be more fish than expected.

The reason was that in collecting the catch before returning, all the fish in the deep-freeze had been removed. Including ours!

But now, finally, to Kingsmill Moore and Ballynahinch. I now cannot remember exactly when it dawned on me how to fish properly, and effectively, for sea trout on that river system during the day. All I know for certain is that the idea came from a specific chapter, "Shanawona and the Greased Line". I also remember certain passages from that chapter which reflect Kingsmill Moore's sensitivity to his surroundings:

"...yet the air was loud with the music of water; water running, water splashing, water tinkling. My companion reminded me that we were now

in the core of the haunted country, and probably on the fairy highroad from Carraroe to Rosses."

The lough was finally reached, and then comes a passage which had painful echoes:

"We were soon afloat, fishing wet-fly in the orthodox methods of the day. Not even a short rise rewarded us, so I changed to dry-fly, casting wherever I saw a white trout rise. They did respond to the dry-fly to the extent of rising, sometimes two or three times, but always missing. I had not learnt at that time that a white trout generally misses a stationary fly and that even a dry-fly is taken best when moved a little.

During lunch I went through my fly-box, selecting a small and very sparsely-dressed wet Orange Grouse ... By the time we were ready to re-start a breath was blowing from the east, enough to move the boat in a barely appreciable drift. Once the fly had alighted it was drawn in slowly, fishing at least six inches under the surface. ... The fish responded to this method at once, taking fiercely with an explosive up-and-down rise. By teatime I had fourteen fish and my companion, a thoroughly competent angler, fishing in the orthodox way had not one."

As those who have been there will remember, the Ballynahinch hotel stretch proceeds in a series of pools with connecting passages. Most of these sections can be comfortably fished from the bank. Applying what Kingsmill Moore had so dramatically described, we had immediate and lasting success. What was particularly satisfying for someone who has a tendency to strike too fast, was how the fish took the fly. The cast moved, by which time the fish was generally on and well hooked.

Another aspect of this approach was that instead of fishing blind, one was mostly fishing to specific rises. This meant that one could fish during the day on most of the beats, especially above Beat One, Beat One itself, and Beat Two. It was very exciting fishing.

As for flies, we varied. We mostly used black flies, very often on double hooks since that ensured fast sinking. Sizes ranged from 10 to 16. We did from time to time experiment with a pattern developed by Arthur Ransome and described in detail by him in his delightful book, *Mainly about Fishing*. This fly, Port & Starboard, was either immediately productive, or provoked no response whatsoever. On occasions when it did work, the fish hooked were generally well above average. One fish which took at the point where the lough flows into Beat One, swam off at great speed out into the lough until it broke the cast. It could well have been a salmon. It never showed.

There were also lighter moments. One afternoon when walking along the drive up to the main entrance, our conversation was interrupted:

"Ach Gott sei Dank. Ihr sprecht Deutsch." ("Oh! Thank God! You speak German.")

This turned out to be a very entertaining Bavarian fisherman who had problems with English. We became very good friends. In real life he was an antique dealer, although he'd originally trained as a civil servant in the German forestry commission. His knowledge of nature was phenomenal, which led to a potentially interesting situation. The hotel is surrounded by woods. Ted went off one day and came back with a large quantity of chanterelles, which in Germany are considered a great delicacy. He strode into the kitchen and asked the chef to prepare these for his dinner. The kitchen staff were horrified, but did as they had been told, also preparing the dish as advised by Ted.

At dinner the dish was brought by the waiter. Ted and my other German friend tucked in. For some reason I turned round. There, stretched round the door, were three heads of kitchen staff staring in the direction of my two friends, obviously expecting to see them drop dead.

One fish, also caught by the method described above, had a very surprising and lasting effect. I was fishing at the end of Beat Two, a narrow channel before a small bridge. Something moved to the fly. I cast again. Something rose but did not take. The third cast resulted in a savage pull. A very fresh silvery grilse of nearly five pounds.

Just as I was netting this fish, the wife of my fishing friend approached. She congratulated me. I suddenly noticed how she kept looking at that fish. I offered it to her. "No, no, no!" she replied, but nevertheless could not keep her eyes off the fish. I suddenly had an idea. This lady also painted, and I had often and appreciatively looked at a picture in her sitting-room. I suggested a swap. She hesitated for a moment, but then accepted my offer. So that now, when I look at that picture, I see not only what is there but am again reminded what reading Kingsmill Moore's book gave me: A wonderfully unique approach to fishing for sea trout under certain special conditions.

A Unique Personality

As I now sit and attempt to gather together my thoughts on Hugh Falkus, all I register is a sudden awareness that what I know of him is limited, and can only be limited. He was such a huge personality that no one friend, however close, could hope to do him justice, or indeed at best do more than recapture those aspects of character Hugh chose to reveal. This may seem a strange statement. Yet I remember so clearly meeting other friends and listening to what they said of him. What they related often bore little similarity to the man I had known for almost twenty years.

One of the equally strange aspects of my personal relationship with Hugh was that since I lived abroad we didn't even meet very often. And yet, for some reason, Hugh spoke directly to me (either in person, but more frequently by letter) in a manner I have experienced with nobody else.

Perhaps it would be better to start at the beginning. I now have the suspicion that even establishing contact with such an unusual and extraordinary personality itself has to be tinged with the odd. There is no way I could have met Hugh in the normal course of events. I'm neither an outstanding angler, nor would any of my professional or other interests have brought us together. In 1978 I was suddenly approached by two journalist friends who said they were fed up with their jobs and that they both fancied going into publishing. Could I suggest any books worth publishing? Or books which ought to be re-published. I immediately thought of Hugh's classic, *Sea-trout Fishing,* and Kingsmill Moore's *A Man May Fish,* which at the time were both out of print. They asked me to write to both authors.

Before describing this first meeting, I would like to try and reassemble my impression of an angler and writer whose talents seemed awesome. Coupled with that was an awareness that even in his books one was in the presence of a person who had lived his life according to his own personal agenda. This was no conventional person, but a man who dictated what should happen – even if, as the biographical sketches indicate – Hugh's life was at the point of death on an astonishing number of occasions. Being of a generation which grew up with field sports, I somehow envied a man who could live a life of shooting, and particularly fishing, to the exclusion of career concerns, even if, as I later learnt, this meant that Hugh had very little money at all over a period of years.

There was also admiration at the way Hugh challenged received opinion. For example, in sea trout fishing, that he refused to stop after dusk had deepened into darkness just because traditionalists maintained that perseverance was pointless. As we now know, continuing to fish on through the night proved that sea trout can be caught, if one adapts to their change in taking habits as the night goes on. This tendency not to accept anything, but to put every aspect of angling to the test, not only brought Hugh new insights into angling practice, but is applicable in other spheres too.

It is somehow so tempting, indeed even reassuring, to do things in a particular way just because received wisdom suggests we should. Such an attitude can lead to a kind of mental blindness. This curious, seeming contradiction in terms is deliberate. For example, it has happened to me that at a particular time of year on a particular river I have fished with a particular fly, because that fly worked in the past. However I remember as if it was yesterday one occasion when fish were rising everywhere, but not taking the fly I offered. It was only after looking more carefully at what was on the water, that I noticed, in addition to the naturals my fly imitated, there were myriads of tiny black flies hatching, on which the trout were feeding.

The very fact of opening one's eyes to what is there, and not only noticing what one expects to be there, can be applied in many different spheres of human activity. For example as a result, in university teaching, I later made a habit of deliberately not giving students too much prior information, sometimes indeed none whatsoever, so that they could approach unknown classical works absolutely uninfluenced. The results were often quite startling, as each generation finds its own priorities in what it reads. Even more surprising, I also found that if I put my mind to it, I could re-read specific texts and nevertheless prevent previous readings from getting in the way of new impressions. All this was the result of having read Hugh's books, and from having listened carefully to what he said to me.

Already, as I try to describe Hugh, I find something strange and completely unintentional happening in that it is somehow impossible to portray this unusual man without consciously, or unconsciously, being forced to bring oneself in as well. Why should that be?

Perhaps because he so stood out from the rest, those with whom he came into contact found they were measuring themselves against him. Not that this was a reaction which Hugh deliberately set out to create. Unless provoked, or perhaps when he was giving lessons in casting. Here I am reminded of two things. Firstly his great generosity. He once invited me for a week-end's tuition in Spey-casting. This would have cost another person £500, something I discovered only when looking more closely at some crossed-out words on a form he sent me. This was at a time when the cancer that was to kill him was progressing. I think he realized that the end was not far away. When we had finished the lesson, he suddenly went over to a long wooden box attached to the wall of his office, took out a very expensive salmon rod, and gave it to me. I was speechless. Not only had he given me his time, but now this wonderful rod as well.

The other "thing" was the lesson. Here for once, and just this once, I experienced a different Hugh. I was first asked if I could roll-cast. I said I thought I could. "Well, do it," barked Hugh. Humiliation then began. "No, no. No! NOT LIKE THAT!" Words I can still hear. This continued. A lesson I shall not forget. Being not only a perfectionist himself, but doing so many things outstandingly well, I fear Hugh did not like seeing anything done badly.

When I think of it now, I smile. I think I was probably inwardly laughing at the time. Underneath that bark, there was actually very little bite. Furthermore, had I persevered, I am sure I would now Spey-cast at least adequately.

After the lesson we went off for lunch. Not to the converted railway station where we had eaten on the first occasion I came to Cragg, as the restaurant there was packed with families on a weekend outing. We drove into Ravenglass, found a pub and went through into the dining-room. The large room was empty apart from two elderly women sitting at the far end. I think they will never forget the experience of having, in a manner of speaking, also had lunch with Hugh. Hugh had his back to the two women. Sitting opposite him I could watch developments. First there was a shy look, and then backs stiffened. Conversation ceased at that table. Hugh's wonderful voice boomed across the restaurant as he launched into reminiscence. Sadly I do not recall much detail. Except that at one stage we started discussing *The Riddle of The Sands.* The action in that classic thriller takes place in an area east of Hamburg on the North German coast. To my great surprise Hugh suddenly began talking about a summer he had spent on a boat in that very part of Germany just before the Second World War. Again my memory lets me down as to what exactly he was doing. I think he was the crew on a rather large sailing boat. Huge numbers of Hamburgers visited this place at the week-end. At one stage Hugh burst into song and, after all those years – more than half a century – gave a rendering in German. The ladies were now definitely and visibly uneasy. But when Hugh then added, with a boisterous laugh: "Yes and every Monday morning the river was awash with condoms," they gathered their possessions and fled.

Although a man who sought solitude and whose spirit and mind grew with exposure to solitude, Hugh could be wonderful in company. He was a great actor, and the world was his stage. In this case he had two audiences: me, and the two ladies. And yet I find myself regretting the use of the word "actor". Acting suggests, or can suggest, putting on an act, doing something which is not yourself. But what if the performance actually is yourself, is you digging deep down inside yourself, to produce something which is genuine? That surely is the secret of both great acting, and great personalities. In the case of Hugh, there's also the tantalizing possibility that there was more than one Hugh. Perhaps each with its own unique identity. After all, if we are honest, each of us is different things to different people.

From a reading of Hugh's books one might – as indeed I had – gain the impression that they were, to use the title of a film I have actually never seen: "The Self-Portrait of a Happy Man". When I met Hugh in

1978, on the surface, he seemed full of life and bursting with optimism. Oddly enough, even the title of that film caused misgivings. Although I was much younger than Hugh, the idea of a life filled with carefree progress towards a happy end sounded just a little too good to be true. Yet this is not to suggest for one moment that what Hugh had committed to paper in his books, or recorded on film, was not genuine. He found great fulfilment in the sports he described and in which he so excelled. But there was a darker side. There had been tragedy in his life, particularly the loss of his second wife who was drowned at sea. He was the only survivor.

This side of Hugh emerged very soon in our letters. He was a wonderful correspondent, whatever he was writing about. Apart from the striking and powerful hand-writing, every word betrayed and revealed the man – right down to the bottom of his soul. Most people, however open they pretend to be, will not reveal all. That was not Hugh's way, once – as those so trusted have testified – he decided you were a friend. This openness, this total frankness in all things, took one by surprise. Sometimes one was really startled. It was nevertheless a privilege and demanded an equally honest response.

Many of our letters were taken up with the matter of writing. Nobody should be fooled into thinking that Hugh's magical lucidity just fell from heaven. He spoke frequently of the struggle:

"*I know how damnably difficult it is – having tried on many occasions and failed every time…*"

As we all know, most of his published work is wonderful. Readable, entertaining, informative, unforgettable. *The Stolen Years,* as literature, as short stories, can be measured against anything published in the last century.

I have in front of me now one letter he wrote very early on in our friendship in which, on one page, he described the beginning, climax, and end of an affair, in unforgettable terms. It started as the result of a bout of depression, something he suffered from intermittently for much of his later life. Here we find him describing himself in destructively brutal terms:

"*… me, the professional toughie, the strong man whose shoulder has been cried on by all his friends – who has never cracked-up – who was* *huddled in the corner, crying with his thumb in his mouth – who quite simply <u>did not know what to do</u>…"*

Spontaneously, in retrospect foolishly, I sent him what I had considered to be a light-hearted play on fishing* and an amusing angling book. Hugh's answer is the most extraordinary letter I have ever received:

Cragg. Friday. 5 a.m.

Dear Jo,

I resolved to stop writing dreary egotistical letters, in fact to stop writing letters at all, and then your new play and a book from Coleby arrived by the same post…!

The play is not playable. And even if it were, not 1% of your audience would understand it. I am not sure that I understand it myself. As for being what you so blithely call an "upcheerer"… I found its intimations of mortality inexpressibly sad. Those silly little men sitting like ghosts in their silly little boat, twisting and writhing and wriggling to change their silly little lives, and emphasizing only that they will retain forever their ghastly sameness … is that "upcheering"? The threat of eternal darkness; the lap of water on the everlasting loch… is that "upcheering"? The chill of loneliness; the terrors of the dark; the dreadful mixture of tears and laughter: the laughter so desperate; the tears flooding the furrows of age like rain on a sodden landscape ploughed by centuries now brittle-boned and thrust back into the soil of a thousand years; ten thousand years; ten times ten thousand … Is that "upcheering"?

Or have I misread the thing? I skimmed through it quickly in the morning… and hastily pushed it into a drawer. In the afternoon, in a despairing effort to stop thinking about that <u>bloody</u> girl (impossible) I took it out again and furtively re-read it. Just now, at four in the morning-after, I sat in bed drinking coffee and whisky and read it again. The bedstead is of iron and very old, with ten brass knobs on railings fore-and –aft. And on every knob sat a raven.

Once at four in the morning there would be only one raven. It sat on my shoulder, and I would shoo it away. After a time shoo-ing wouldn't shift it, so I killed it. But it came back from the dead with one of his mates… Then

---

* See **Fine & Far Off** on page 99.

with two; then three; then four. And now there are ten of them and they huddle, preening, all along the bedrails one on every knob. And they croak.

And this morning, just now, not an hour since, as I read your manuscript for the last time, they reminded me that on the Spey a fortnight ago I sensed suddenly that I was making my final cast; that I no longer cared whether I rose a fish; that there was no more pleasure in it for me. And as my fly swung round on its last journey and I slowly wound in the forty yards of white Number 11, DTF, the clacking Hardy Marquess Salmon Number 2 seemed to echo the awful clacking emptiness of my own mind.

It was nice of you to send me Hillaby's book. Very nice. It's so full of pith; so well-written. But it depresses me. I no longer find its humour humorous.

"Let there be a bonfire of angling books", I said aloud. "And a roasting of anglers. Let their clacking voices, like their clacking reels, be silent." And the ravens cackled in chorus and croaked: "Silence will come soon enough!"

Yours ever –

Hugh

This letter was written at five o'clock in the morning, after a night of sleepless misery. And yet the text, to use another of Hugh's memorable phrases, appears "to have been written in blood." He is still in the depths of despair over the end of an affair. However the image of "ravens" refers back to the death of his second wife for which he was never able to forgive himself although he was in no way responsible. The ravens were a recurrent nightmare. Of course not only was it foolish of me to have sent what I did, it was also insensitive. Yet for once an act of foolishness provoked a matchless piece of prose. A letter which can be read for all time. Only much later did I realize that in saying what seems to be so damning, Hugh was in essence paying me a huge compliment. In case this might seem to be not only self-deceiving, but downright masochistic, I must point out that this little one-act play had originally been conceived as a not very serious discussion of what grown men are up to when they take a boat and ghillie and go fishing on a lough. That Hugh should have discovered so much seriousness surprised me and, at a much later date, gave me great encouragement.

What in all fairness needs adding here is that a day or so later Hugh wrote an apology, a most fulsome and – as far as I was concerned – completely unnecessary apology. Indeed, one of his many wonderful qualities was to say exactly what he thought. This rather un-English practice I always found both refreshing and rewarding. It meant we could talk about things openly, with complete frankness, and know that we were discussing an essence and excluding the personal. I've known very few people with whom it has been possible to converse on any given topic in such a way that complete frankness did not interfere with, or cause a breach in personal friendship.

I am realizing increasingly just how fragmented and incomplete this attempted portrayal of Hugh Falkus has become. But how could it be otherwise? When I met Hugh he was already 61 and my visits to Cragg were few and far between. I also realize that in spite of having threatened to, I have not got round to describing that first visit and first meeting. I think that this is no longer appropriate. The initial impression merely confirmed what I had expected. It was the communication with such an unusual character, the insights into an often unhappy man, the exchange of views on a variety of subjects, and the sense of privilege at having been permitted to share a little time with Hugh Falkus which were of much greater importance. And it is not as if he has left us completely. His writings are still there. Every page reveals the essence of a rare and scintillating personality.

II

Aegina

Dear Philip,

After you have read this letter I want you to destroy it, and, should we meet on some occasion in the future, don't ever refer to it. But I have just got to tell somebody what I have gone through. I cannot live alone with it any longer. God knows, I am not very strong but the last months would have shattered someone with the constitution of an ox. I feel as if my whole personality has been taken out piece by piece, examined and thrown away, leaving just a physical presence behind.

I am writing to you for a number of reasons: you do after all know me well and you are a person who is able to keep secrets. You may even want to write. Don't! Just putting pen to paper is already helping me, although in talking to you I put myself into your hands. You live a long way away and we are unlikely to see each other for years. By then the immediacy of this experience will have passed – I hope – and so there will be no embarrassment or distress on either side.

Of course you still haven't the faintest idea what I am talking about. I have never liked talking about myself and hate being forced to face facts. I thought I had even managed to stop thinking about myself.

But let me start at the beginning. Just after we met last autumn I set off on my research trip. I am very sorry that I have not written all these months, since I know you wanted to hear about what I was doing. You may find this hard to believe, but even at the very start I was unable to communicate with anyone outside the valley, for reasons which remain incomprehensible to me. Now that I have left, it seems as if my mind is attempting to close the time-gap created by those months. While I was there I found it increasingly difficult to think back to the outside world, and now I am away from it, it becomes more and more of a struggle to make my mind return to this subject, in spite of the melancholy and depression which are a direct result of it. It is curious: I can at the moment almost see my mind visually, as little streamers of tissue stretching out to link up and close for ever this episode in my life. In fact I find more and more that I consider myself as a being apart, that I no longer belong to the body and personality I once inhabited. As a scientist I am intrigued: as a human being, I am frightened. To give you an example of what I was just saying; when I was in the valley, I could not for the life of me, remember how it was I first learned of its existence. Yet now, writing to you, it comes back instantly. For it was in your house that I happened to open one of your magazines at a page on which there was an article about the valley. At the time I had been looking for an area which had remained untouched by modern agricultural methods, so that I could carry out some comparative studies on insect life in limestone regions. And, as further investigation showed, this was the perfect location. As I write these lines I am taken back in time to that warm afternoon in May, the first really fine day of the year. I sat down on the chair facing the open windows in your lounge and looked down your garden across that quiet Oxfordshire valley – I still cannot understand how you could bear to sell that lovely house and go abroad again – and I was relieved when I saw that I should not even have to travel too far, and also, much more important, that the language spoken there was one in which I had some fluency. So, in a roundabout way, you are responsible for what happened; but you mustn't think that I blame you in any way. Further reading and investigation proved the correctness of my first impressions and in November of last year I set off just for a few weeks to have a first look around.

To my dying day I shall never forget how the valley looked that morning. I had been driving hard for three days, and, as I arrived in the area late in the evening, I decided not to go on that night but to stay in a village on the other side of the mountains. As it turned out, this was a sensible decision since the roads, which had become worse and worse, were simply dreadful over the mountain. The wine I had in the evening probably caused me to oversleep and it was nearly ten o'clock before I left the little guest house and drove slowly up the road which was really no more than a rough track.

Up and up I drove, avoiding ruts and boulders, some of which were quite large enough to have put the car out of action for good. It took some time to reach the top; the clouds became thicker all the way up. I drove slowly down the other side, using the gears as an additional brake until I was clear of the cloud. One moment I was surrounded by swirling cloud, and the next I was in sunshine. I stopped and gazed down, switching off the engine as I did so. There was a slight suspicion of wind at this height: down in the valley nothing moved. Nothing, that is, except for the coils of autumn mist unravelling on the sides of the valley. It might have been smoke, but the smoke from the chimneys in the tiny hamlet below went straight up. There was not a sound; not the bark of a dog, not the crow of a cock; nothing, just the gentle push of wind against my cheek at the open window. From this altitude I could follow the river's course from one end of the valley to the other. All along its length, smaller channels led off in a series of loops which looked too regular to be natural. I sat there for quite fifteen minutes listening to the wind. It looked like a toy island wrapped in cotton-wool.

I drove on down to the village. Actually there were only twenty houses and the number of people living there amounted to a hundred or so. Just away from the houses on a slight elevation stood the ruins of what once must have been a fine house. I was told that it had belonged to a local aristocratic family and had been burned down at the end of the war. Apart from this there was nothing to suggest that anything had changed in the valley for centuries. I am not going to attempt to describe things in detail. You know I am not much good at it, but I'd like you to try and imagine the scene for yourself.

Of course my appearance on the mountain road had been immediately noticed and there was quite a crowd, consisting mostly of children, awaiting my arrival. Children are always curious, but on this occasion I had the feeling that they looked at me as if I was some sort of bizarre object, solid enough, but completely beyond what they would normally expect to see, and thus not quite real. This must sound crazy to you, because although the valley is off the beaten track, it is by no means completely cut off from civilisation. There are plenty of visitors in the summer, too, who come for the fishing, or just to walk. I was the first stranger to come during the autumn and I suppose they found that a little odd.

I had an introduction to the water-bailiff and was taken to his house. It seemed to be full of young girls. One of them took me through the house to the back. I ought to have mentioned that this was the last house in the village and behind it the slope led straight up the mountain. Of course I had read all about it, but it still came as something of a shock to see the spring. Certainly, 'spring' seems an odd word to use in this context, for it was a pool fifty yards long and about twenty wide; from this, enough water flowed to form the river. As so often happens in limestone areas, it trickles away to nothing at the end of the valley, to reappear again many miles to the south:

As I approached the pool, I banged my leg painfully against a trestle on which a large black metal tank rested. 'He's not here', the girl cried, 'he'll be down at the spawning beds. It's not far. Can we take the car?' she asked shyly. We drove through the hamlet and out along the bumpy track through the meadows, until we came to a bridge over one of the feeder-streams. In the shallows I saw more large trout than I had ever seen in my life before. It was an amazing sight. Since the water was so clear, the fish seemed to be floating on air above the white pebbles, until in a sudden flurry they sent the water flying.

A little way along the stream were three people, one of them in the water. My attention was attracted from the first to the man in the water, a giant of a fellow, over six and a half feet in height. He was bent almost double to take out fish, stripping them of their spawn into containers on the bank. However it wasn't this which so fascinated me, but the way he did his work – so much so that it was some moments before I tried to catch the attention of the others there. Large people are often clumsy, but this man was a marvel of physical coordination. His ability to take the fish from the water, strip them of their spawn and return them was done with such rhythm and smoothness that his huge hands appeared to be breathing life into those invisible specks of creation.

You must forgive my mentioning these seeming irrelevancies but I do want you to have some idea of the surroundings, and particularly of this man. You will thus perhaps appreciate better what happened later.

The giant straightened up, groaning slightly as he did so. His eyes did not change expression when they met mine, for he was totally absorbed. Even when he became aware of my presence, his gaze was more inward than outward. Spaosu, the bailiff and fishery-manager, shook me warmly by the hand and introduced me to the third person, his daughter, Gina. She stood up and regarded me with that open, unashamed curiosity one often encounters in children. In an adult it is singularly embarrassing, at least to somebody like me. She did not speak and immediately sank back to her original sitting position on a wooden stump. Up till that moment I had not been able to see her face since her long hair had completely covered her features. She too was very tall, though perfectly proportioned, and, as I later learned, only nineteen. It is absolutely no use my trying to describe her. You can never describe somebody you love – or hate. You think you can, because an image pursues you constantly, relentlessly. If you try to turn this into words, the individual features dissolve and change almost kaleidoscopically.

The first time I hardly even saw her. Her eyes stabbed into me and all I felt for the moment was the pain. I remained standing there, looking at her for seconds after she had turned her attention elsewhere. The giant remained where he was in the water, and went back to his work again. Spaosu apologised for not having met me when I arrived and invited me to visit his house that evening.

I stayed at the house of a widow in a room above the stable, although animals were no longer kept there. I arranged to take the room again on my return next summer. I intended to remain for several months in order to complete my studies of the aquatic insect life in the valley. During this first visit I rambled along the river and the many small streams which had been made to flow round the meadows. The channels had been so constructed that they could be opened in places to irrigate the fields.

Oh, I almost forgot to mention one other person who later was to have a major, if not the major, part to play in what happened: Rhea, Spaosu's wife. It was easy to see to which side of the family the daughter owed her appearance. Physically, Gina was magnificent: of her other qualities, I shall speak later.

Spaosu told me that Rhea had never really forgiven him for taking her away from the city. Her feeling of superiority to the women of the hamlet had not made life easier for either of them. As the years passed she had become withdrawn, brooding on what might have been, and, according to Spaosu, rather letting things slide. The children, never having been checked or properly taught, had run wild. Spaosu himself was far too good-natured to assert his authority, and was now more interested in the welfare of his fishery than in the fate of his children – particularly since both his sons had been killed in the war. Gina, who often went with him while he was working, was the only one for whom he seemed to have any great regard. But I am forgetting the giant. Nobody knew what his real name was. He had been left there by refugees after the war and had grown up in the village. The community was so small and remote that it was rather like a large family. Sonnio, that's the name which had been given to the giant, had been more or less adopted by the village. Spaosu was very good to the boy when he discovered his love of the river. As a child he would play contentedly on the bank all day, touching the water with a kind of childish reverence, and, as he grew older, assimilating all its ways and wiles.

He knew where the big trout lay, where pike were likely to be found, when the eels ran; the man's mind was the dictionary of the river. Open it at the right place and there was the answer to any question. Of course it was not quite as simple as that, for he did not find it easy to put into words the knowledge he had acquired. He had hated formal school and had played truant as often as he was able. He combined the knowledge of a man with the mind of a child, but for me he was both guide and teacher.

Since Spaosu rarely walked far it was Sonnio who most often accompanied me. But the older man was often able to help me since he could look back on nearly fifty years of work at the fishery. His reputation was such that even when the present regime came to power he was allowed to remain at his post although he had been working for and had been on good terms with the old landowners.

My few days soon passed and I was often at their house. Rhea was polite, but never did more than courtesy to a stranger demanded after she discovered the purpose of my visit. She hated the river with a steady undiminishing passion. Concern for the health of the river had kept her husband in the valley all his life and she knew he would never leave it. Sonnio was the only one who could wring a smile from Rhea. Not that he ever spoke much. Away from the river, his personality changed. He stooped, shambled, and was unsure of himself in company. The children would have made fun of him openly – they often did behind his back – had they dared. One of my lasting memories of Sonnio is of him walking away from me on the last evening. It was cold and he was wearing an ancient black coat which had originally been made for a man much smaller. His great hands hung down inches below the end of the sleeves, the long fingers stretching and curling as if he had no control over them.

As for Gina, she never made the slightest attempt to notice me: my greetings were ignored. In any case she came and went just as the whim took her. The family seemed used to this.

As you know, I returned to the valley in April. During the day I would go out alone, or with Sonnio. I generally took with me bread, cheese and local red wine for my lunch, eating something more substantial in the evening, cooked by the widow. Why do I mention these things? Perhaps you will think my mind is going. Maybe it is: but you must try and see the valley and my daily existence. Since my work progressed well, it would have been reasonable to assume that I was, yes, happy. The weather could not have been pleasanter, the sun becoming hotter with each successive day. The lack of rain did not matter. The sluices on the channels were opened to flood the meadows, the water eventually finding its way back into the river.

Sonnio was somehow different. It was not that he was unfriendly or anything like that. He had become more inhibited, more uncertain of himself. He would mutter to himself and clench those fists of his till the bones crackled. Once beside the river though, he became his old self again. He talked quietly, gently, struggling to tell me what I wished to know. His eyes were never still. He had a knack of looking along the river and immediately noticing anything unusual; a movement, a ripple on the water, a stunted fish, or one which had not recovered from spawning. These fish often kept close to the bank out of the current. I have seen him take these trout with his bare hands, almost charming them out of the water. When he wanted to, he seemed somehow to be able to fade into and become part of his surroundings. Sonnio always carried a spear with him, the wooden shaft ending in a long, brightly-polished barbed tip. He told me that he had practised since youth and, as he often demonstrated, he had attained a deadly accuracy. Sometimes he would swing his huge body up into a riverside tree and crawl out along a branch. From this vantage point he would look into the clear green water below. Once or twice I clambered up beside him and from there he showed me where a pike had hidden itself so that it was invisible from the bank. He then stepped down again, quietly approached the spot and hurled the spear into the river. I never saw him miss.

Sonnio was not the only person who had changed in those few months. Spaosu and Rhea now treated him coldly. He was not invited into the house any more. And Gina? She laughed and mocked at Sonnio whenever she saw him. More than once I saw her flaunting herself in front of him when she thought nobody could see. In her eyes I was nobody, so I suppose she thought my seeing this did not matter. And yet you know, I had the uneasy feeling that she was trying to goad Sonnio into becoming jealous of me, but he was too involved in his own misery to react to such subtleties. As the weeks went by I became more and more aware of the strain under which he was living. Although his eyes were normally curiously bereft of expression, to me, watching him so closely, it was obvious that the poor fellow was half-crazed by his love for Gina. Those who love, I suppose, always see these signs.

There was one place along the river-bank to which I often went. I had boards out in the centre of the stream, under which insects laid their eggs. I took these out regularly for examination. It was also a good place to take fish when I needed to. I made a point of studying the stomachs of trout which either I or Sonnio caught. A punt was kept here, so that I could cross the river if necessary. Often I worked there for hours at a time, sitting on an old rotten stump and using a box as table. In this shady spot behind the bushes I was invisible to anyone on the opposite bank. After I had been coming here for a time Gina suddenly appeared one evening and swam in the ice-cold water not fifteen yards away from me. Philip, I tell you, that girl's body was so beautiful. And she knew it. She held me there, an unwilling observer. Unwilling ... no, if I am honest, I could not say that. What really upset me more than anything else was the slow realisation that she was revelling in the situation of having a secret admirer.

What followed was worse. One night in the last week, of May I awakened suddenly. A candle was burning on the bedside table. In front of it and facing me stood Gina. When she saw that I was awake, she took off the coat she had been wearing. Under it she had only a thin night-dress. She looked at me as she had done that first day, twisting the knives in the wound. She bent forward, her eyes still holding mine.

'You're a man aren't you?' she hissed.

Although I was too overcome to reply, I must have nodded.

'Then prove it.' she said.

She let her nightdress slip to the ground, and remained standing where she was so that I could see her before snuffing the candle and getting into the bed.

Philip, that Gina wasn't a woman, she was a witch, and what's more, I think she hated men. She took me. I cannot describe it otherwise; afterwards tossing me aside, humiliated, emptied, shrivelled. When she had finished with me, she rose from the bed and left without a word. I lay motionless, hardly breathing, mentally and physically petrified. I must have fallen asleep eventually because the widow had to knock for some moments in the morning before I answered. I forced myself to get up, and tried to continue with my work. I must have done so, although I now have no clear recollection of the days that followed. I was glad to return to my seat on the river bank where I could sit alone. Gina did not come back. I assumed that she had finished her game with me.

The weather was superb and the whole valley was a mass of lush green and flowers. The birds sang from morning to night. I am not a very romantic person at the best of times, but even in this state of suspended shock, I felt the surge of generation going on all around me. During the week after Gina had come to my room I hardly saw Sonnio – for which, as you can well imagine, I was not sorry. When I did, he was always busy – furiously busy – it seemed to me.

I was sitting in my usual place one evening at about five o'clock. The atmosphere was heavy, the heat oppressive, and a storm was rumbling behind the hills. The hatch of Mayfly was late – no doubt a result of the heatwave – and I had a feeling that the storm might bring about this annual miracle. It is a sight which always amazes me and I wished to see it on a river which I now knew to be free of any kind of pollution. Sonnio was standing on the other side of the river, his spear held ready. He had obviously seen a pike in the weed and was waiting for it to move. The willows, swaying slightly, cast a pattern of shadows across his bare shoulders and chest. It was very still, apart from the occasional sound of distant thunder. No fish were rising and even the birds had been silenced by the heat.

Suddenly there was a splash in front of Sonnio. I looked up; he looked up, uncomprehendingly. A hot puff of wind ruffled the surface of the water. Gina was just behind Sonnio. She had a willow branch in her right hand, pressed against the top of her bathing costume. She threw it over his head into the water, in a cruel mime of his spear-throwing, and laughed at him. He sprang at her. Normally she would have been too quick for him, but not on this occasion. Physically they were a good match, and she fought hard. But this time Sonnio was not cowed. He took such a grasp on her as made her gasp and hurled her to the ground.

Large single drops of rain started to fall. While those two, locked at first in battle and then in the act of love, did what they had to on the other side, the Mayfly came out all along the river. The smooth surface was shattered as trout surged, plunged, in their attempts to take hatching or landing insects.

The air became white as myriads of insects emerged for their brief nuptial flight. It was like a snowstorm except that the snow, instead of coming down, rose, and then danced, high above the river. The air was so thick with insects that the two figures on the opposite bank became blurred and indistinct. Seagulls, swallows and swifts dived and screamed as they caught the hapless insects. Then, as the rain came down in torrents, the hatch ceased as suddenly as it had begun. The clouds hanging heavy over the mountains brought dusk with them; lightning flickered on the wet gleaming bodies of the lovers. Yes, lovers. I began to understand certain things at this moment. Some people might have called what had happened, rape. But of whom?

I was no longer alone. Spaosu was standing a little to my right, bent forward slightly as he peered across the river. He was no more than six or seven yards from me. How long he had been there I do not know. As I looked at his face, I realised slowly that it was not so much anger that I could read there, but something else. Suddenly he clambered into the punt, almost overturning it in his frenzy. He paddled across the river, shouting wildly as he did so. Sonnio heard him, sat up, looking round to make out where the sounds came from. When he saw Spaosu, he sprang to his feet and snatched up his spear.

'Get back!' he roared, 'she's mine!' Gina lay where she was and did not move.

'She's not!' screamed Spaosu. 'I'll kill you!'

Sonnio did not answer. His spear flashed in the lightning and I heard it strike. The old man remained seated at the back of the punt for a moment. He tried to rise to his feet, shuddered horribly, and then fell, lying grotesquely across the punt. I could now see that the spear had passed through his leg, impaling him to the boat which, having lost its momentum, slowly swung out into the stream.

Gina got up and would have run forward. Sonnio stopped her. 'He's dead: let him go!' He released her arm, turned, strode away while Gina sank to the ground, where she lay motionless.

I rose from my seat and walked away, through the rain. Hours later I found myself in the village again. I went straight to bed. When I awoke late the next morning, it was still raining. The puddles in the single street grew larger and larger. Down the mountain, most of which was how hidden in cloud, water was tumbling. From hour to hour, trickles grew into torrents: in the meadows, where the hay was ripening, small lakes formed. From the widow I learned that Spaosu had been found and carried to the house. When Gina did not come back, people had gone to look for her. She had been lying unconscious beside the river and was now in a high fever. Of Sonnio, nothing was known. It cannot have been difficult for Rhea to guess the reason for her husband's fatal heart attack. Apparently she had said nothing but had picked him up and taken him to her room. Late that night she had been seen to go out in the rain.

I felt weak and remained in bed all day, sleeping fitfully and waking occasionally from bad dreams, although I no longer know what I dreamt.

The rain stopped during the night. When I looked out of my window in the morning I could see people standing beside the river, pointing and gesticulating. I dressed and went down to see what it was all about.

As I approached the group, I could see what they were looking at. Fish. Dead and dying fish. Everywhere one looked were the grey-white bellies of dead fish, bobbing slightly in the slow flow of the waters. The seagulls were back. Again they were diving and searching as they picked up fish from the surface of the water. There was nothing I could do. I returned to my room and sat there waiting, thinking. Later that day, I was roused from my thoughts by the sound of breaking glass. Below my window, a dead seagull lay on the ground. Other gulls, flying above the houses, were doing strange things. As I watched, one dived, or rather fell, into the water, flapped once or twice, and was still. Another crashed into the wall of a neighbouring house. I drank heavily that afternoon.

When I awoke the following morning, the hamlet seemed unusually quiet. I missed the sound of children, of dogs barking, of chickens. From my window I looked out again across the valley. The early morning mists were lifting and I could see that the floods had receded somewhat. I was surprised that my breakfast had not been brought up, for the widow was normally very punctual. I found her sitting in the kitchen. She had just heard the news.

Sonnio had returned the evening before. He had walked into Spaosu's house and had gone straight upstairs to Rhea's room. She wasn't there. He found her standing beside Gina's bed. According to the widow, he had picked Rhea up and hurled her through the window. She was killed instantly. He had walked out of the house again and into the hills.

Gina died the same day.

There was nothing I or anybody else could do until the floods subsided. While waiting I sat in my room, or walked by myself round the marooned village. Animals and chickens died suddenly and violently. Nobody was drinking the water any more. People stayed in their houses, waiting. It took a week before the road was clear. Each day I could walk a little further, although it became more and more frightening to do so. There was such silence. The only sound was the sound of one's feet, sinking into the muddy ooze. Not a cricket chirped, the birds had left, the vegetation was dying. And the smell of those fish rotting in the sun; shall I ever lose my remembrance of that?

On my last morning in that dreadful place, my wanderings took me to the spring. It was then that I noticed the black metal tank against which I had stumbled shortly after my arrival. It lay on its side beside the water. Spaosu had once mentioned to me the weed-killer he had bought some years previously, and which it had been so difficult to transport to the village. God only knows what terrible chemical changes had taken place in its composition since then. But how had the contents of that tank got into the spring?

Suddenly I remembered Rhea's walk in the night. She had always hated the river....

As I Lay

Up they came every morning from under the window sill. Fishing boats moving slowly out across empty water. I watched from my bed. A broken column of black smoke went out with them, remained after they had passed from sight.

I was standing at the top of the beach. Early morning in April. I shivered in spite of the extra clothes. The stones on the beach were wet, from rain or spray. They looked cold. Down below, the sea stirred; a dirty brown swell. Grating shingle, audible from where I stood. There was cloud; possibly rain further out.

'Think you can be here by six-thirty' the man had said. Well, here I was, hoping they hadn't left without me. Some boats had already gone.

The boy in the hut was bent over two flat boxes. He grinned as I entered.

'Can't think what's happened to the boss this morning. He's very late.'

'That's good,' I said, 'I thought I was.'

'No, you're all right.'

He bent again over the tray of frozen sprats. He picked one up, pressed the point of a large hook into the eye of the fish which slowly twisted as the iron went through the body. Small flakes of ice came off, dropped to the floor. The boy's finger's were red, raw. I sat down. Row upon neat row of baited hooks lay silver in the second box. They were attached, on short lengths of braided nylon, to a long line.

'Rather a cold old job,' I said.

'You get used to it.'

'I suppose you've been at it a long time.'

'Oh no, not so long. Couldn't stick, inside work.'

'It must be pretty tough all the same.'

'Oh, you get used to it.'

The boss came into the hut, tugging on a bright orange oilskin.

'Morning,' he said, 'must have overslept. We'd better get a move on ... do the rest on the way out.' He nodded in the direction of the bait boxes.

We went out to the boat which was resting on blocks beside the hut. I left the loading to them. They knew what to do. The open boat slid down the beach over greased sleepers. At the water, the boss told me to jump in, or I'd get wet. I clambered in over the high edge of the boat, sat on the centre seat by the engine. One of the other boats was waiting. A man threw a rope which the boy tied to a ring on the front. The boss and the boy stood behind the boat, pushed it down the last part of the slope into the water. They waded a few steps, jumped on the back end. There they hung for a moment, neither in nor out. They pulled themselves over the side. The boat had begun to swing round as the tow-rope tightened. The boy took hold of the starting handle, strained to swing it. The engine suddenly caught after a few turns. The boy went to the front, cast off the tow, waved to the other men. I remained on the seat in the middle. The wood vibrated through my whole body. The beat of the engine came through the rusty exhaust pipe like the quick firing of a gun.

The boss baited the remaining coils of line, stopping occasionally to put a hand inside the top of his oilskin trousers. The wind caught the thin curls above his forehead; his light-blue eyes wept with the cold. When he had finished, he took the tiller again, sat inertly, staring ahead. We seemed to be moving very slowly. Away from the shore there was little swell. The boat rose slightly with a wave, slid down again. Occasional splashes of spray came cold against the face. The noise of the engine made conversation difficult. My hands thrust deep into inside pockets, I tried to keep warm.

The boy unwrapped his breakfast, began to eat. He passed me a cup of coffee. It was not hot, but sweet and weak. He offered me a sandwich. I shook my head. I had eaten before coming out. He took off his oilskin jacket. Although we were well out to sea, we appeared only to have travelled a few hundred yards parallel to the land. Three other boats were still level with us, no longer very near. I could make out the shapes of the men standing up in the boats. I pushed my hands under my pullover, hard against the shirt. Slowly, very slowly, warmth returned to my hands.

The sky lightened, a misty cold-looking day. Spots of rain blew against my cheeks. The little wind was in our faces. We kept on straight out for nearly an hour, always within sight of the land. The boat did not move very fast.

We approached a red buoy. Right in front of it, the boat turned sharply to the left almost as if we had reached the junction of a road. Soon after, a smaller buoy showed above the swell.

The boss pointed.

'That's where we start,' he said.

'Are we in for a good day?' I asked.

'We might,' he answered, 'it hasn't been too bad the last week.'

I went to the other side of the boat, out of the way. The boy was rummaging around at the front, looking for something. He lifted out a short thick piece of wood with a metal hook at the end. He grabbed the buoy, which he heaved into the boat and quickly untied the end of the line.

'We've got about a mile of line down,' the boss said. He switched the engine into neutral. The boat hardly rocked. The boy started to draw in the line, his elbows going backwards and forwards fast. The boat gave a jerk as the boss put the engine into gear again. He took in the line at the back, coiling it into the boxes. He shook out the tangles, his movements smooth, unhurried. The line came in. At first, no fish. Just empty hooks. From some, small pieces of uneaten sprat still hung. The boss flicked them against the edge of the boat. Gulls gathered overhead, dipping and diving ceaselessly.

Their cries rose above the noise of the engine. The boy pulled in the line fast. Small fish he swung straight into the boat, crashing them against the front seat. The hooks came away, tearing the mouths. The fish fell to the floor. They moved their broken mouths, flapped against the wood. The boy took the gaff to the larger fish. The bottom of the boat filled slowly. The fish were mostly cod. Some large flatfish. Skate, the man told me. It was the other fish which caught my attention. The eyes. Pale green, opaque. Dogfish. With the large fin down the back, blunt heads, they looked like small sharks.

From time to time, the two changed places. The boss pulled in the line less jerkily, his greater height making the work easier. The front section of the boat slowly filled with fish; alive, slowly dying.

We came to the end. The new line was fastened to the marker buoy, tossed overboard. The boss stood at the back, twirling the line out of the flat boxes with a stick. The lead on the line took it straight under the water.

The gulls had remained with us, picking up sprats, occasionally a fish which dropped off as it was hauled in.

The boy took out a knife to clean the fish. I sat with the boss at the back.

'Nasty creatures, gulls,' he said.

'That's a job I don't much like,' he continued.

The boy had just opened one of the dogfish. Four or five baby ones moved weakly on the board. Their eyes too, were that strange milky green.

'Extraordinary, isn't it,' the boss said. 'Dogfish don't lay eggs. The little ones come like that. Nasty creatures, gulls,' he repeated, as the boy emptied the tray over the side.

'Do you know, sometimes in winter the little birds come and land on the boat, so tired they can hardly hang on. God knows how far they've travelled. The gulls wait for them. They must get thousands.'

'Have you always been a fisherman?'

'Yes,' he replied. 'Runs in the family. It's a mug's game these days. The big boys are the ones who make the money.

Trawlers. They clean up everything in the nets.'

'Would you fancy another job?'

'Don't know, really. I doubt it. Lucky to have the boy. Aren't many who're prepared to put in the hours these days. We're out nearly every day of the year. Bloody cold it is, sometimes, I can tell you.'

'I can well imagine,' I said.

'You'd better hop up the front again, if you don't want a wetting. Jump out, the moment we touch.'...

'OK,' I said.

One of the other men was waiting with the rope. The boss and the boy pushed the boat out of the water. The drum at the top of the beach started to turn. We held the boat steady as it was hauled up the beach, pushed in the blocks at the top to hold it.

Several women already stood outside the hut, waiting.

The boy threw the fish into metal tubs, turned a hose on them. The tubs filled with water, light red in colour. He emptied the tubs, took the fish into the hut. He passed me standing beside the boat.

'Well,' he said, 'you going to sign on?'

'It's a tough old job,' I replied.

'You could be right there,' he said.

Sweet Chavender

Water slid from the sculls, was quickly swallowed by the current. The rowlocks squeaked as he lifted the sculls out of the water, as he bent forward again. He grunted at the end of each stroke, a grunt which was more of a dry bark than a grunt. Soon he settled into his accustomed rhythm, the boat moved forward jerkily. The bow dipped as he pulled, a ripple went out at both sides, smoothed away as the current caught it. He bent forward, pulled; bent forward, pulled; the boat moved slowly against the current. He worked his way steadily, a few yards out from the cement wall at the bottom of the river bank, towards the next slip. The rowing-boats, roped together in bunches, rocked slightly as he passed. It was end of season. The sign 'BOATS FOR HIRE' had slipped over sideways. From the river all he could see was 'BOATS FOR …' The sun came out for a moment, its light reflecting off the dull brick of a factory end-wall. He'd caught fish there.

He rowed on, keeping close to the bank where the current was not so strong. Occasionaly his scull caught the muddy end of a willow branch hanging down into the water. Once, the bloated body of a cat floated past, grey skin showing beneath the matted fur. He broke his rhythm for a moment to avoid hitting it. Slowly upriver. On the other side a woman was walking with her dog. Too far away for him to be able to see her face. For a while they moved more or less together. She sat down on a bench while the dog played round her.

He stopped rowing again. A barge passed, low in the water. He turned the boat sideways, held it steady as the wash came; it lifted the boat. The throb of the engines carried through the water, thudding through the boards below him. As the wash subsided, he brought the boat to face upstream, bent to the oars once more.

At this point the trees and bushes were thick on both sides of the river. On the right, behind them rose the roofs of houses. He could hear the traffic as he kept the boat on its slow upriver course. The traffic sounds faded again as he approached the next bend, disappeared when he turned it. He was nearly there.

He stopped rowing opposite the tannery. The wind – what wind there was – was blowing away from him. There was no smell. Two hundred yards further on children were splashing about in the shallow water of a bay, throwing sticks and stones for a dog.

He lifted out the sculls, laid them inside the boat. He dropped the anchor down, hand over hand, making no disturbance in the water. The boat slipped sideways until the rope tightened. There was enough current here to hold it steady. He stepped carefully over the seat, holding the side for balance, sat down again to face in the other direction. He remained thus for some minutes, breathing hard. He coughed, spat into the water. The blob of spittle floated away, rising and falling in the ripples caused by his movements in the boat. He put his rod together, pushing it away from him as he did so. He went through the same motions to thread the line through the rings. From a tin box on the floor-boards he took a made-up cast. As he picked up the thick red-and-white float, the single lead weight slid down the cast, bounced on the boards.

He looked carefully at the hook, ran the point across the nail of his thumb on which it left a tiny white groove. He coughed. Bending, he felt in his old canvas bag for the cheese. Hard, yellow cheese, old, strong-smelling.

He broke off a lump, kneaded it between his hands. The cheese crumbled into flaky pieces. Slowly it became softer as he rubbed it between his fingers and thumbs. He pressed the hook into the cheese, moulding it round the hook. It was a large lump. After wiping his hands on his trousers he lifted the rod. There was no need to adjust the float; he had been there before. The bait plopped into the water, sank immediately. The float was carried away by the current. It stopped, went under. He raised the rod, met resistance under water. He bent forward, pulled. Something moved at the end of the line, came slowly towards the surface. An old rusty tin showed above the water for a second; the hook came away as the tin rolled over, making a bulge in the water. The tin sank from sight again.

He reeled in, laid the rod down. There had been quite a disturbance in the water. On examining the hook, he found that the point had broken off. He tied on a new hook, dropped the cast on the boards, felt in the bag for his sandwiches. As he bit into the bread he could still smell the bait-cheese on his hand. He glanced towards the near bank. At the end of the swim, a backwater had formed round the trunk of a tree jammed into the clay bank. A raft of objects had collected, all pressed together: plastic bottles, twigs, a large white rubber ball, feathers, a boot, leaves. An occasional eddy swirled the whole mass.

A bell on the tannery roof rang out. He looked round. Figures emerged from the door facing the river. Some ran towards the bicycle sheds; the women moved briskly in the direction of the main gate. The bell stopped ringing. Voices came over the river to him although he could not understand the words.

Within a few minutes the yard was empty. Except for one man who was pushing the big gate shut. He walked back again, slamming the door as he entered the building. The sound carried over the river.

He put more cheese on the hook, picked up the rod. The bait dropped into the water. He let the line pass through his fingers, keeping a slight hold as it ran out. The float showed clearly above the brown oily water. He let the float go away from him for quite some way, held it steady. A tiny ripple went out at both sides of the float as the water divided round it. The float swung to the right and left as the current shifted. He sat there, hunched forward; the rod in his right hand, the line lightly checked between finger and thumb of the left. The cigarette in his mouth burned down slowly. He spat it into the water. It hissed, went out. He coughed, reeled in. The bait had gone. He lit another cigarette, baited the hook, cast.

Half-way down the swim the float stopped. It jerked sideways, went under, for a second leaving a hole in the surface of the water. He waited, struck. Line went out fast, disappearing into the brown water. At the end of the first run he held harder. There was no need for care, it was not a big fish. He lifted the fish over the side, taking the line in his hand. He removed the hook, tossed the fish into the bottom of the boat. Its tail smacked flat against the floor-boards. The mouth opened and shut. He was not looking. He wiped his hand on a rag, put more cheese on the hook, cast.

Another fish pulled the float under almost immediately. A bigger one. This too he brought quickly to the side of the boat, pushed the net under it. He gripped the fish hard round the middle of its body. The big mouth opened. The fish made a dry sound, almost like a bark. He took out the hook, threw the fish down with the other one. Another cast. Soon there were fish all over the bottom of the boat, none of them entirely still.

The shadows lengthened across the river. He put another cigarette in his mouth, sat motionlessly in the boat. Water ran off the chain, down the inside of the boat as he raised the anchor, rested it a moment on the gunwale before heaving it into the boat. He sat down again, coughed.

The sculls dug in hard against the current, the boat moved downstream fast. The sun went off the water. A light mist rose off the surface of the river, he could see his breath. On down the river. The boat slid away from him at each stroke. Hard at the beginning, the sculls cutting into the water. He went quickly downstream.

He turned the boat across the river as he approached the landing-stage. The water slapped against the underside, he pulled harder till the boat faced upstream. He eased the boat in towards the float, brought it in against the pieces of black tyre nailed to the side. He stepped out, holding on to the mooring-rope. One of the cats came towards him, rubbed hard against his leg, went to the edge of the float. It miaowed, turned to look up at him.

He held the boat out, glanced round behind him. The other two cats came bounding down the bank. He drew the boat in slowly. The cats jumped in. Each caught up a fish in its jaws. The cats left the boat, ran up the bank again, with the fish-tails dragging along the ground.

He secured the boat, took out his things, leaving the other fish in the bottom of he boat. He walked to the top of the bank, stood looking down the river in the gathering darkness. Somewhere near him he could hear one of the cats eating a fish.

Day-Flies

The second day. I slowed down along the bumpy earth track. At the end there was just room to put the car in the shade of a tree. Dust blew past the open window. The wind rushed by: smoothing, flattening swathes of high grass in the meadows like wide lengths of rippling silk. The sun, already hot, was burning up the last of the morning haze.

I opened the back of the car. How the women in the shop had laughed as I attempted to explain what I wanted. Not that they had very much; not even butter. I had just pointed. They had packed what I required in rough grey paper bags. I laid the food in the grass where it would keep cool. The bottle of wine I pushed down into the river where the reeds were thick enough to prevent it from being carried away by the current. I returned to the car, took out what I would be needing. I drew on my thigh boots, adjusting the straps over my shoulders so that I could move easily. I picked up the other things, set off for where I intended to begin. I felt the sun warming the canvas of the waders. It would be good to enter the water. I moderated my pace, taking more leisurely strides. The long grass whipped against my legs: a dry sound. It was almost the only sound. Almost. Somewhere in the depths of the grass, the grating cry of a corncrake went along with me. Like the whirr-whirr of a sewing-machine. All the long week that sound never left me. It was not even a particularly pleasant sound yet it did not irritate. And always tantalisingly near. Not once did I see that tiny crouching bird which I knew only from pictures. One evening a corncrake called just a few yards away from me at the point of an island in the river. I walked up and down, trying to find it. The bird stopped calling once or twice while another took up the cry on the far bank. I did not see it.

I walked on, more slowly, no longer tired after the long journey. The river was not visible from any distance. It meandered through the valley between high banks. On three sides of the valley, steep fir-covered slopes. The village lay on the fourth, behind me. I glanced back. The tall slender red steeple of the church stood out clearly on the hillside; beside it the dark walls of the graveyard.

I walked more slowly as I approached the river. The wind caught the willows and alders along the banks, blowing hard in my face, ruffling the surface of the water. I knew where I wanted to go. A startled pigeon flew almost into my face, went out low across the field, swerving right and left.

I kept away from the edge of the bank as I reached a long bend in the river. This was where I intended to begin.

The river ran deep here so that it was not possible to enter the water. I approached a thick bush, moved slowly to the edge. From this point I could see across the river. My dark glasses took away the glitter on the surface. I stood very still. The grayling would be lying deep in the water, resting like shadows against the bed of the river, moving slightly in the underwater currents. The clear water was dark-green in the deeper parts. Rings formed, widened on the top of the water as fish came up from the depths to take flies on the surface.

I watched. Mostly small fish. I was not going to cause unnecessary disturbance this time. It was still early. I could return later. I stepped backwards, not fast, until I was away from the river bank. I wandered on to a place further along. There was no cover at this point. I had to go down on my knees, working my way forward through the ripe grass. I took in the sharp fresh smell of crushed herbs. Meadow flowers brushed against my cheeks. Drops of perspiration ran down my face, steaming the glasses. I remained kneeling, took out a handkerchief, wiped the glasses clean.

I knew what I was looking for. I had to cast right across the river. Kneeling as I was, it was not easy to put out the line so far. I lifted the rod, moved the rod backwards and forwards. Each time I pushed the rod forward I released more line, carefully, unhurried. I was excited, but it was not the excitement of the day before. The line, with the tiny artificial fly on the end, came to rest on the water. It was almost too far for me to see. I reacted when I saw a movement on the surface. A small grayling. Not the one I had wanted.

I pulled in line. The fish suddenly jumped out of the water, tugged wildly. I looked again. A pike, also not large but larger than the grayling, was right behind. The pike followed fast but seemed undecided, as if it was puzzled at the grayling's behaviour. I took in line, wishing to spare the grayling. The pike appeared to make up its mind. It swung away, turned back to fasten on to the grayling at the side, taking the grayling halfway down the back. Both fish went down. I could no longer see them. Instead of one, I was now holding two fish. They came up again. The grayling broke free: momentarily. The pike closed in once more. I held hard, drawing both fish towards me.

Something gave. The line came back.

I could see both fish as they went down for the last time. They sank from sight. This was not what I had intended. I sat back on my heels, stretched out my legs, sat down properly. I watched for some minutes. I could see no signs of movement in the river before me. I rose to my feet, walked slowly back to where I had begun; a long ripple of rough water in the middle of the river where two currents crossed.

That was where I had lost a good fish the day before. I had been too hasty. Because of surface disturbance it was not possible, even with the glasses, to see down into the water. The fish was still there. I saw it break the surface, go back down again. The fish rose several times as I stood beside the bush, watching. I was going to do things better this time. If he comes, I'm going to wait, I said. I'm going to wait. I gauged the distance, deliberately taking time. I held the line in the air, coordinating my movements until rod, line and fish appeared for a second above the surface, disappeared. A huge head. Not even very far from me. I glanced round, changed my position so that I could throw the line behind me without catching in the trees.

The fly was on the water, moving over the spot where I had last seen the fish. I drew in line as the fly came towards me. I lifted the line off the water, held the fly in my hand, blew on the fly to keep it dry, waited. The surface broke, burst, throwing out waves some yards to the right of where 1 had seen the fish. Again that violence as the fish went down. I cast. Come on, fish, I said, come on.

As if responding, the fish went for the fly. I waited, raised the rod. A moment, a fraction of a second. Off, out into the river he went.

Charging through the weedbeds. Going, going, going. He stopped, changed direction. I stood still, giving line when I had to; taking in when I could. I could not hurry the fish in the heavy weed. I had to think, try to anticipate. The minutes passed, the fish rushed less. I gained line. I saw him in the clear water, coming nearer each time he passed me.

I held the net under the water. He was in the net, struggling. A final quiver ran the length of the fish's body as I laid it out on the bank, still in the net. I pulled back the meshes to look. A big trout. Not young, already past its prime. The body not as fat as it should have been. It was time.

I swung the bag over my shoulders, walked along the bank, back to the car. I bent down, shook off my waders. I went down the bank. Walking was now so easy. I lifted the bottle out of the river. Cold drops of water ran off my hand. Sitting down in the grass, I picked up the knife, cut thick slices off the loaf. They felt soft and moist. I raised the bottle. The wine was so cold that at first I couldn't taste it. Just a cold, tingling sensation as I swallowed. I peeled the rind from the cheese, broke off a piece, ate it with the bread.

I sat on in the grass, with the sun shining down on me, eating, drinking wine. The wind blew against my face, still cooling.

A Deeply Objective Fairy Tale

Once upon a time – say, until about twenty years ago – there was a beautiful river which meandered through beautiful unspoiled countryside. The water, which flowed down from a huge reservoir, was crystal clear and cold; so cold, a perfect habitat for the many kinds of fish which thrived in this unspoiled stream. Sadly there were also men. Humans. Mostly from the city. They wished to share in this paradise. So all along the banks of this beautiful river they reserved sections where they could stay. With their caravans, their tents, their dogs, their children, and their disturbance of erstwhile peace.

The children and adults played and swam in the river, throwing stones, making noise where there had previously been nothing but the sound of birds and water. The dogs barked, chased animals and birds, also fouling the banks with what dogs do.

Then something happened to the water. It was no longer quite so clear, quite so pure. Men had again interfered, by introducing invisible but poisonous substances, because local politicians did not wish to spend money on filtering effluent before it entered the river. Soon, at certain times of the year, the river bed became covered in thick brown slime. Plants could not grow, insects suffocated, the sun's rays could not penetrate this brown sludge and the river began to die.

Then more city ideas were put into practice, because people are so much more important than nature. Nature has no genuine lobby. Nature just suffers and dies. Slowly. Or fast. Nature does not know the word compromise. Pathways were created along both banks, so that cyclists in droves could speed through what had been a bird sanctuary.

Later city-dwellers started coming in ever greater numbers, with their canoes and paddle- boats. Not only disturbing the river, but also tearing out plants on their way down the river.

There had always been anglers, who came, made no noise, fished occasionally, but who kept a watchful eye on the river. They struggled to look after the river and its rightful occupants.

And then, largely because of laws made by men who foolishly believe that nature today will still find its own balance, cormorants – birds which have no natural enemies – were declared a protected species; so that on this river where there had been none, suddenly there were, at certain seasons, hundreds. The river is now almost totally devoid of fish.

With the result that what was once upon a time, now really *is* once upon a time. This river which was formerly so beautiful, so pure, so unspoiled, is now just one more playground for human beings who want to play but not pay. Or think. Or preserve. Or think any further than the weekend ahead. And that is the end of this deeply objective fairy tale.

A Morning in Northern Ireland

When he took the shotgun out of the case he immediately noticed that the barrels needed oiling. Automatically he first reached for the ramrod, afterwards wiping an oily rag along the blue-black metal before slipping the gun back into its case. He put it away, beside his own.

He sat down, coughed, pulled out cigarette paper and began to roll tobacco. Having lit up, he settled back in his chair and looked out unseeingly across the waters of the lough.

"We know where your son is," they had said. He could still hear the rattle of boots on the gravel as they moved off. They had not come back. He would have been ready the next time. They knew that. His ears would have registered the telltale sounds.

The dog at his feet stared up at him, eyes full of interest, as if waiting for something to happen.

The big man heaved himself up, straightened, and went towards the door, motioning to the dog that there was to be no noise. As they went along the hallway he slowed briefly as he passed the door behind which his wife would be sitting.

From the rack beside the front door he lifted the rod, already made up. Outside, a chill wind ruffled his thinning hair before he pulled on a cap. The big black dog padded beside him as they went down towards the lough, occasionally looking up to the man. The dog stopped when a bird rose out of the grass. The man moved on, making no sign.

They came to the shore. There were two boats, one roped to a ring attached to the boards of the jetty, the other just showing above the surface. There was an area of calm water between the two sides just showing. The man did not even glance at the sunken boat. The dog jumped into the boat beside the jetty while the man untied the rope, got in, before automatically loosening the petrol cap. There was a slight hiss of released air. The man turned, took on board the rod and fishing bags. With an oar he pushed the boat out before starting the motor.

The boat cut cleanly through the surface ripple, waves spreading behind as the boat picked up speed. The man sat in the stern, his attention concentrated on what lay ahead, no longer even registering the rush of cold air against his face.

He was thinking of the boy. They had gone out like this so many times. The father calm, the boy eager to be out there. The dog stood, with two feet resting on the bow planking, always eager to see what lay ahead.

Within a short time they reached the island. There was a line of calm water where the ripples ended in the shelter of the trees. The man switched off the engine, let the boat slide forward as it slowed and slowed. His attention was fixed on the water ahead. Nothing seemed to be moving. Perhaps it was too early. He had plenty of time. Automatically he reached into his pocket for a cigarette, lit it without taking his eyes off the water. It had suddenly gone very quiet. The wind seemed to be dying away, as it sometimes will.

The sun showed briefly. The man looked up. From where he was he could see the church on the hill. The stone, white, was clearly visible, glinting then fading as clouds caused the light of the sun to go away.

What had the papers said: … much loved by both communities … a sense of shock … of loss … a policeman committed to the pursuit of justice." It was known who had committed this act. No witnesses had come forward.

It was even said that the killer had passed in front of the church on the day of the funeral.

The man thought briefly back to his wife sitting, as she so often did, alone in that room behind a closed door. He shut his eyes for a moment.

He sensed something, looked up automatically. A ring showed in the surface, widened. The man remained motionless. Perhaps something was about to happen. But he had time. So much time. In fact he had all the time in the world.

Achilles Heel

It was one of those days. We had been out all morning and the rain had never stopped, or eased. We were both a little under the weather. One of those times when you wonder why you do it. I said as much to Tom, who just laughed.

"Well you keep coming back," he said.

"What about lunch?" I replied.

"May as well. The fish don't seem to like the rain either."

He brought us to the shore, clambered into the water and pulled the boat up over the rocks. He waited to help me.

"Careful now! It's slippery."

"Thank you, I'm not as steady on my feet as I once was."

"Ah, you do pretty well, and you've been at it longer than most."

Tom took out the bags, went up to the hut on the island where we generally stop in the middle of the day. He had a fire going in minutes. We took off wet coats and sat in the hut, waiting for the warmth to get through.

"Why do we do it?" I repeated. "More to the point, why do you do it? And you live here!"

"That's why," Tom said. "That's why I'm here," he continued, nodding in the direction of the lough.

"But you're not local."

I looked at him. He was so young, or seemed young to me. Yet I knew he was already in his late thirties. A powerful figure, he looked even bulkier in the clothes he was wearing. I always felt comfortable when out with him. He was never flustered, as if nothing could take him by surprise. A great comfort on lakes where conditions can change suddenly.

"No, but I've been living here for as long as you've been coming." That was very true. He had offered to take me out on my first visit, and we had continued fishing together ever since.

"There's nothing quite like these big loughs," he went on, "they're wild, really wild. They don't give in easily. You have to live with them, study them constantly, always have them in mind. In all their strangeness. That's the challenge."

"But you can't fish all the time."

"I don't."

"And?"

"Well, I can still be thinking. I follow the moods of the lake, like you would with a person."

"Identification?"

"Ah, it's not easy finding words. I mean it's different when I'm out with other people. Then I have to think of them – and *for* them often enough."

"I should hope so."

"Oh, I didn't mean you. We're friends. I can relax with a friend."

I had never really thought about our relationship. At least not like that. Two weeks a year is not a long time. Yet very intense. Day after day, sharing a boat, with everything that can happen in boats. Whims of weather. Catching fish. Or not catching fish. Being in a favourable spot. Being out when things are happening. On big lakes little can be taken for granted which, I suppose, is part of the fascination.

"It's different when I'm by myself."

"Oh, why?"

"Because I'm by myself. There's just me, the elements, and what I'm after."

"But you come from the city."

"That's just it. I couldn't stand being in cities any more. It all got on top of me. I had to get away."

"But from what you've told me, you were not alone."

"You mean my girlfriend?"

"Of course."

He paused. "I suppose she will never understand."

"Did you ever discuss the matter?"

"It was pretty hopeless. She never liked me fishing anyway."

"Her rival."

"I suppose you could put it like that."

"Actually, worse than a rival."

"What do you mean?"

"She might have won … against another woman."

"You could be right there," he murmured expressionlessly, continuing to stare out into the lake. "But what about yourself? You keep coming."

"That's different."

"Why is it so different. You once told me it was to get away."

"At the beginning, it was."

"You had a wife."

"You know that."

"Yes, but you left her."

"Yes, eventually I left her."

"Ever regret it?"

"No."

"Well, there you are."

"Ah, but with me it was different."

"As you said. But why?"

"I was unhappy. Desperately unhappy. Were you?"

"I begin to see what you're getting at. No… I wasn't unhappy…"

"But?"

"I had this yearning. To be alone. Untied. So I could live this through."

"This?"

I looked at him. The same indefinable something in his expression. I thought back to what I knew of him. In essence not very much. Small surface details. Like his work, for example. He restored furniture, antique furniture. I had never actually seen him at his work – I don't think he would have welcomed that – but I had seen the results. In his workshop. It was amazing that such huge hands could perform such delicate operations. He had to show me precisely what it was that had been restored, because his work was executed so perfectly. Perfection. A difficult word, since perfection implies a total exclusion, permitting, or allowing for no weakness. Perhaps "beauty" would be more appropriate, because beauty is visible, can be felt, is almost indefinable.

"Now don't get me wrong. I like my work. Restoring gives me huge satisfaction. It means I can be my own boss. I'm totally independent. And there are big challenges to face in what I do. Very often you have to puzzle and puzzle before you find the right way of making any given piece of furniture, after treatment, look as it should. Genuine. And I genuinely enjoy that. But it is nevertheless a limited satisfaction. At least for me.

Whereas out on the lake, however much you think you know, you never stop suddenly facing situations in which whatever you thought you knew doesn't work, situations which will defeat you. And that's a very different challenge … one which never ends."

"But fish, even big fish, have brains the size of a pea."

"I knew you would say something like that. Can you not be serious?"

"Perhaps I was being serious."

And who knows, perhaps I was being serious. Perhaps I was also putting the question to myself! Perhaps I was approaching a sense of personal inadequacy, because Tom was so good at everything he did. For example, being out in a boat with him meant accepting his superiority. Anything I achieved was achieved largely because of what he made possible. And everything he did was somehow just right. If he was casting a fly, for instance, every movement seemed calculated – no, not calculated – was naturally synchronised to achieve the greatest effect with a minimum of physical effort. I could only watch in admiration, without ever having the slightest suspicion that what he did was done to impress. He was always too much absorbed in what he was doing to leave any room for personal vanity.

"So this activity … this obsession … has in fact given you what you felt you were missing out on. In your earlier life?"

"I have never really attempted to define what it is finally … ultimately."

"Could you?"

"I'm not sure. I imagine – now that you put it to me – it has to be that what I experience out here on the lake is a feeling that you never reach the end, that essentially you never get beyond the beginning. With the road stretching out there ahead of you."

"And that makes you happy."

"That's a big word."

"You haven't answered my question."

"Can one?"

"You could try. For example, your private life. What about … personal relations."

"That too is not an easy question."

"Well, there must be women around. Even here."

"Of course there are."

"And?"

"They seem to have different expectations. I mean I'm not talking about casual encounters. And of course most in my age group are already married, or have moved away."

"And the younger ones?"

"They have a different … agenda. I suppose I must seem old. To them."

"And your old girlfriend?"

"She would never live here."

"But you have established something. You have an aim, a challenge that will – to use your words – never go away."

"Do you know something," Tom suddenly said, "I think the rain is easing. There's even a bit of light in that sky. I think we should be getting back on to the lough. We've a lot to catch up on."

Fine *and* Far Off

Cast

Denis: late seventies, retired army office
Bill: late sixties, also retired
Jamie: boatman. Perhaps in his forties

Great care should be taken over the speed of delivery. Passages of almost ritual slowness alternate with sections of fast abrasive staccato. In places, rhythmical musical accompaniment would be conceivable. Jamie's diction should avoid standard English but not be geographically identifiable. The repetitive 'sir' all through is not to be stressed but should flow naturally.

Stage Directions

As in the production directed by Manfred Roth ('Klappmaul Theater') at the Frankfurter Hof Hotel, Frankfurt.

Denis and Bill wear dinner jackets, carry rods (no longer than 4 feet), short lines and flies made from pipe cleaners and feathers, thigh boots (Bill), wellingtons (Denis), bags; Jamie in rough sweater, black trousers, rubber boots, with net and picnic basket.

On the set two tables, one long, one short. It is important that the tables together should give Jamie enough space to sit on the table-top and go through the motions of rowing without seeming to be too crowded in by the two men. Both tables covered with bottles (empty and started), glasses, as if a party has just ended. Two armchairs and a smallish coffee table on one side of the stage to which Denis and Bill first go, putting their fishing tackle down. Jamie will have to clear the debris from the tables. Music should be played until the dialogue begins. ('Tea for Two', e.g.).

Denis has a brightly coloured stuffed fish, with perhaps the tail sticking out of his one boot. Jamie goes first to Denis, who fumbles for money while Bill sits staring into the audience, not moving. James then approaches Bill, sticks out his hand. Bill looks at the hand, glares round at Denis, reluctantly hands over a note. Bill then stands up, starts putting on his gear. He removes his jacket and slips on a fishing waistcoat. Denis keeps his jacket on. Denis goes to the centre of the stage, looks at one table, decides it is not long enough, indicates as much to Jamie. He then stares pointedly at Bill who unwillingly goes over (one thigh boot on, the other foot in a stocking) and helps Jamie to bring the tables together.

Denis goes off stage to bring in the fourth man to whom he gives the fish which the audience, but not Bill, can see. This man then sits under the table with a copy of the script (concealed between the covers of Spectator or some other serious journal). The man has nothing to say, but is Denis's stooge, to wake him up, catch the line when fish are hooked. Bill should never register that he is aware of the fourth man's presence. The two men get ready. Jamie puts a chair on one end of the table and helps Denis up. Denis sits. Jamie then supports Bill as he too climbs on to the table. At the beginning Jamie should sit with his back to Bill. Jamie ties a rope to one of the table legs, and jumps up on the table, noticing angrily that a cushion he has put there for himself has disappeared. Denis has taken it when Bill is helped on board. Jamie leans over the table and pulls on the rope until the anchor (which till then should have been concealed from the audience) is on the table. Jamie sits down, the music stops, he begins to row and the dialogue begins.

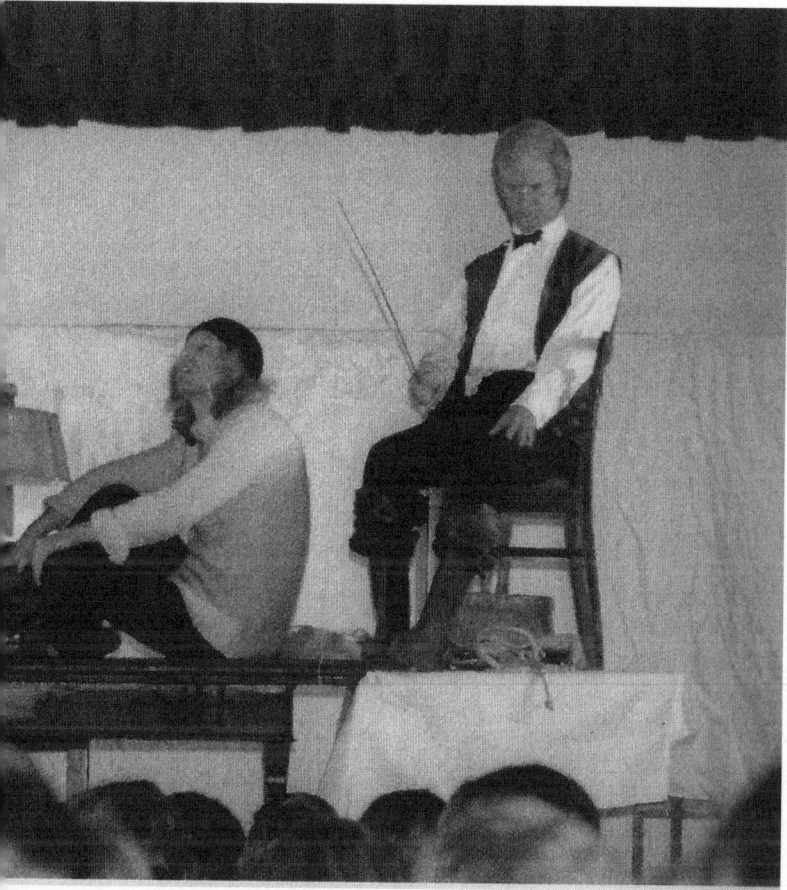

      The cushion trick can be repeated later when the two men change places. Jamie first takes back his cushion when they stand up. Bill seems to stumble, grabbinng Jamie, pulling Jamie half up. Denis snatches the cushion, leaving Jamie to fall back on the hard table-top. When the last words have been spoken the beginning of Schubert's 'Trout' Quintet could be played, loud, and at a speed of 45 instead of 33.

Bill: Are we going to have a good day, Jamie?

Jamie: A good day, sir?

Bill: That's right.

Jamie: *(looks round)* We could do, sir.

Bill: You really think so?

Jamie: Sir, you never know your luck.

Denis: Eh, what's that?

Bill: I was asking our... our friend here if he thought we'd be having a good day.

Denis: Oh ... and what did he say?

Bill: He said we could do.

Denis: Hmph ... did he, by God!
I don't like the look of the sky.
It's gone very black.

Bill: It has. What do you think, Jamie?

Jamie: Well, it's not as bright as it was, sir.

Bill: Is that bad?

Jamie: It's not always good, sir.

Bill: There's plenty of wind, though.

Jamie: Oh yes, sir. There is wind. God bless it.

Bill: You need wind, don't you.

Jamie: Oh, you do, sir.

Denis: What's that?

Bill: I was discussing the wind. It's east, isn't it?

Denis: Touch of north, I'd say.

Bill: What do you say, Jamie?

Jamie: There is some north in it, sir, but from the feel of the boat, I'd say there's a bite of east as well.

Bill: Will that bring the fish up?

Jamie: You never know with fish, sir.

Denis: I never like a north wind, in the boat.

Bill: Our boatman says there's some east in it.

Denis: It's damn cold; I never like it when it's cold.

Bill: Oh, I don't know: I remember some good days.

Denis: Not when it was like this: there's a feel about the wind.

Bill: What do you think, Jamie?

Jamie: Well sir, it is blowing.

Bill: What sort of flies can you recommend, Jamie.

Jamie: Flies, sir?

Bill: Yes, I haven't fished this lake before.

Jamie: Now I had a gentleman with me yesterday.

Bill: Ah!

Jamie: He put on black flies, nothing but black flies, swore absolutely by them.

Bill: Did he catch anything?

Jamie: Oh no, sir! But he had great faith.

Denis: You've got to know what you're doing.
I know: I've fished before.

Jamie: I'm sure you have, sir.

Denis: You'll get fish if you do what you know.

Bill: But you didn't like the weather.

Denis: Ah! Weather's one thing; what you do another.

Jamie: Very true, sir.

Bill: I'd have thought they went hand in hand.

Denis: You play your own hand:
You've got to know what you're doing.

Bill: I think I know what I'm doing.

Denis: What was that – you do mumble so!

Jamie: The gentleman said he knew what he was doing, sir.

Denis: Does he, by God. I worked these things out years ago.
Size up conditions, act accordingly.
Confidence! That's the word.

Jamie: Sure, faith is a great thing, sir.

Denis: By the way, what about the sandwiches.
Did they put them in the bag?

Jamie: I think so.

Denis: What do you mean, you think so? Have a look, man.

Bill: It's all right.

Denis: And the net?

Jamie: The net is here sir, I've got the net.

Denis: That's something. I say, did you bring your little bottle?

Bill: I did.

Be a good chap, and pass it down, will you.
Denis: Nothing like a nip before you start.
Jamie: Very true, sir.
(passing bottle but not being offered anything)
Bill: What happened to yours?
Denis: Mine? Oh, I must have left it in the hotel.
(passes bottle back)
Bill: *(muttered)* You would.
Denis: *(to Jamie)* What'd he say?
Jamie: I'm not sure I understood, sir.
Denis: Now, have you checked your knots?
Bill: I think so.
Denis: It's no good thinking, man; you must know!
Knots are the link,
and a tenuous link,
between you, and what you're after.
The proverbial chain
is as strong only
as its weakest link.
The links are the knots.
You tie the knots,
so it's you
for the make
or the break
in the link.
Bill: What knots do you use, Jamie?
Jamie: Ah, sir, there's knots and knots.
I've seen many knots in my time.
Denis: Nonsense! There's only one knot.
You know that, Bill. The one I tie.
Bill: Indeed I do. But it has let me down. On occasion.
Denis: Never! Never. Not once in thirty years has that knot let
me down. No! There was once.
I once let a fool of a girl tie the knot… it slipped.
That's not a mistake you make twice.
Jamie: Right, sir!

Denis: I say, what about a snifter before we start.

 Bill: I'm sorry, I missed what you said.

Jamie: He said he'd like a little something before we start, sir.

 Bill: You just had one.

Denis: Did I? … So I did. Well, just to chase away the cold.

Jamie: It is cold this morning, sir.

Denis: Thanks. Will you have one?

 Bill: Not just now. It's a little early for me.

Denis: Aah, it's the one thing that picks me up.

We're not getting any younger, *(puts bottle down at feet)*

 Bill: No *(sour)*.

Denis: Now then, boatman, where are we going?

Jamie: Not much further, sir, not much further.

It's a devil; with this wind.

 Bill: But better than a flat calm.

Jamie: Oh, you're right, there, sir.

Denis: The cloud's lifted; just a little.

Jamie: Who would have thought it, sir.

 Bill: I've got a feeling we might have some fun.

Jamie: You'll have the fun, sir.

Denis: What about here?

This shore looks good,

we can drift all down

with the wind at our back.

Was this what you had in mind?

Jamie: We can start here, sir.

You never know, you just never know.

Denis: Now don't you forget.

Hold the boat steady,

just off this shore.

Jamie: Oh, I'm the steady one, sir.

Have no fears, I'll take you down

to the end of the lake.

 Bill: Looks good enough to me.

Denis: To business.

(starts casting. Both begin. Stiff, mechanical movements with right arms, from the elbow. Will need careful synchronising for real effect)

Bill: It's a bit awkward casting, with this wind.

Denis: You wait and see.

It's not the line but where you put it.

Sometimes the fish are near the boat, but won't take well. Then you've got to cast out.

Bill: Hell! *(has caught boatman's hat)* Very sorry.

Jamie: That's all right, sir, *(removing hook from hat)* it's an old hat.

Denis: Can't you be more careful.

After all these years.

Bill: Wind caught it.

It's not easy to control the line.

Denis: You ought to know better.

Bill: I saw a rise.

Jamie: You did, sir?

Bill: Indeed I did. Over there!

Jamie: Over there, sir.

Bill: Yes, over there!

Jamie: I'll get the boat over.

Bill: Yes, get the boat over.

Denis: Hey, don't turn the boat over. I just saw a fish.

Bill: Yes, so did I. Where was yours?

Denis: Just over you.

Bill: And I saw one too, just over you.

Jamie: That's the fish, sir. *(Bill strikes)*

Bill: He missed the fly.

Jamie: He didn't get it, sir.

Denis: You struck too quickly.

Bill: Too quickly?

Denis: Too quickly.

Bill: I don't think so, it was not a proper take.

Denis: You gave him no chance.

Bill: But you saw the swirl.

Denis: I saw the swirl, a fish on the take.

Bill: But he didn't.

Denis: You did the taking, right away from him.

Bill: It banged on his nose. He couldn't miss.

Denis: No good on his nose.

Bill: That fish came short, he never took the fly.

Now Jamie, you tell me, did I miss it, or was it the fish?

Jamie: Ah sir, now you're asking.

Bill: Are they bad takers, Jamie?

Jamie: They're sometimes not easy, sir.

Denis: *(muttering to Jamie)* He struck too quickly. Didn't he?

Jamie: He's a very fast striker, sir.

Bill: I'm quick on the take, Jamie, always have been.

Jamie: Never a faster, sir.

Denis: *(still in an undertone)* Bloody fool missed it.

Bill: Ah, got one. At last.

(stands up, much activity now. Line held by stooge)

It's a good one!

Jamie: Oh, sir, it is.

Denis: Now, hold him. Don't let him go.

Bill: Get the boat round. He's coming in fast.

Denis: Use your rod, man.

Bill: Phew! That was near *(fish misses front of boat)*.

Jamie: Yes, sir, nearly he was under the keel.

Bill: Just look at the line, he must be a size.

Jamie: Oh, yes, sir.

Denis: Come on, come on, the longer they're on the quicker they're... *(stooge lets go)*

Bill: Damn! *(sits down hard, rocking the boat. Fish off)*

Denis: Watch what you're doing, man.

You'll wreck the boat.

Bill: How on earth did that happen?

He just came off.

Jamie: He just came off *(quietly)*.

Denis: You took too long.

I hold mine hard.

It looked to me as if
that fish played you!

Bill: What is one to do with a biggish fish?

Denis: You show him who's master.

Jamie: That's a funny thing, sir.

Denis: They soon learn.
Cow them! Give'em some stick.
(clenches fist to emphasize his words)

Bill: Sometimes the hook just comes out.

Jamie: That can happen, sir.

Denis: Not if you hook them well, before you begin.
I say, do pass the bottle.

Jamie: It's down at your feet, sir.

Denis: Oh, er, is it? *(takes a swig)*

Bill: I think that I now could do with a drop.

Denis: Boatman, would you pass that down.

Jamie: Very good, sir.
(passes, looks longingly. Pause as they drink).

Denis: Now then, this is no good.
We must do something.
(both cast, get their lines tangled)

Denis: Hell! Can't you watch what you're at?!

Jamie: Not to worry, sir. I'll untangle the knots.

Bill: That wind!
I have a feeling
it's one of those days.

Denis: I've no time for that kind of excuse.
There are no bad days:
there's just bad fishing.

Bill: Have you never experienced a time when you're off.

Denis: Of course, but I don't put it down to fate.
It was my fault. That's what.

Bill: Ooh! What are these fish doing.
(wild strike, hat falls off, caught by Jamie in net).

Jamie: Here you are, sir.

Denis: He missed it again, *(muttered)*

Jamie: You think so, sir.

Denis: I know. He always does.

Jamie: Is that so, sir.

Denis: It's enough to drive one to drink.

          I say, Bill, how about another little drop.

          It'll bring you luck.

Bill: I thought you didn't believe in luck.

Denis: *(slowly)* I suppose no one really knows.

Bill: There's another.

Jamie: What's that, sir?

Bill: Hey, Denis!

Denis: Wh… what!

Bill: You see that?

Denis: What? Where?

Bill: A fish.

Denis: That's no fish.

Bill: It's not a rock.

Denis: Sometimes you get on my hump,

          all that excitement about nothing at all.

Bill: It was just like a lump,

          up through the waves.

Jamie: This lake's very deceiving, sir.

          Sometimes the light shines in the strangest of ways.

Bill: I'm not easily deceived.

Jamie: Could be, sir, but them fish is deceiving creatures.

Denis: Damn! *(strikes)*

Bill: He took short. I told you so.

Denis: He never took: opened his mouth, wide, like a door, I
          could see it.

          As if he was yawning: never came anywhere near the
          fly.

Bill: Just like mine. You wouldn't believe me.

Denis: No, nothing like yours.

          (to boatman) He missed his.

Jamie: Is that right, sir?

Denis: I know: he always does.

Bill: What do you mean, it wasn't like yours?

Denis: Now yours was a boil, a definite boil.

Bill: A boil?

Denis: Yes, a boil, it was quite clear to me.
Made a hole in the water, as he went down.
My fish missed the fly, turned down beside it.

Bill: I don't think you struck.

Denis: A big one will hook himself,
you've got to give him time.

Bill: But mine was a fast one.

Denis: You're the fast one. Isn't he, boatman?

Jamie: Very fast, sir, never a faster.

Denis: There! You see. *(hooks one)*
That's what I mean.
That's my boy *(stands up)*.
That is a big fish. Oops!
(boat rocks, as fish is played: fish taken all round boat,
the other two bending to get out of the way.
Fish possibly circling, with J. & B. bobbing and ducking
to get out of the way of the line. J. nets fish, which has
again been held by stooge)

Jamie: Now that's a fish, sir.

Denis: Not bad, not bad. He'll go three pounds.

Bill: Nearer two, I'd say.

Denis: No, no, no. A good three.

Bill: Some fish weigh light.

Denis: Look at him, man, there's depth in those flanks.
All muscle and thrust.

Jamie: A grand fish, sir.

Denis: Now, what'll he go?

Jamie: Oh, two … to three pounds, sir.
No doubt of that.

Denis: You see!

Bill: You'll always get the odd fish that makes no mistake.

Denis: No mistake at all. You saw that.

Bill: I saw it all right. Look out!

Denis: What! *(looking away from line)*

  Bill: A fish.

Denis: Damn! You distracted me.

  Bill: What do you mean?

Denis: You shouted.

  Bill: Of course I shouted: you had a take!

Denis: Well, how was I to know, with all that noise?

  Bill: I just wanted to help.

Denis: I don't need your help. Was it any size, boatman?

Jamie: It was a fish, sir.

  Bill: Do you know something?

Denis: What?

  Bill: I think the rises are coming to you, at your end of the
boat.

  What about a change?

  A change would be fair.

Denis: Doesn't make a scrap of difference

  but, we can change if you must.

  I don't like changes, they upset the rhythm,

  there's nothing like rhythm, when you're out in the boat.

Jamie: You have a point there, sir.

  Bill: I'd like a change.

Jamie: Very good, sir.

Denis: Oh, well, I suppose we'd better.

Jamie: Right, sir, now for the change, but watch how you go,
and don't rock the boat.

  I'll do my best to hold her steady.

  *(both men clutch each other over the head of the
boatman, executing a clumsy, prolonged dance, before
they get past each other. In the next section Denis
should remain motionless, or should only make
occasional casts, leaving attention focused on the other
two)*

  Bill: Now the wind's gone away.

  (dialogue slows down here)

Jamie: But it's not quite so dark, sir.

Denis: I told you, warned you
about changing things round.

Bill: I don't think I follow quite
what you mean.

Denis: There's far more to it
than meets the eye.

Jamie: Sir, the eye is mortal,
that's what it is.

Bill: Is it magic, you mean?

Jamie: Ah, sir, who can tell?

Bill: Tell me, Jamie, do you fish, yourself?

Jamie: Oh, no, sir! That's not for me.

Bill: Not your sort of thing?

Jamie: That's what it could be, sir.

Bill: Or d'you not have the time?

Jamie: Sir, there is always time.

Bill: *(looking round, shivering)* It must be cold here in winter.

Jamie: It's not warm, sir.

Bill: What do you do when the season is over?
D'you farm?

Jamie: You could put it that way, sir.

Bill: A lot of work round here?

Jamie: *(slowly)* There is work, sir. Always there is work.

Bill: Plenty to do?

Jamie: Oh, lord, yes.

Bill: Jobs?

Jamie: Now, that's a question, sir.
There's plenty here when the summer is done
that are, you know, available.

Bill: Ah, yes. You have a family, I suppose.

Jamie: Oh, yes, sir.

Bill: Children?

Jamie: You mean, am I wed?

Bill: Yes.

Jamie: Ah! But you're the married man, sir.

Bill: Me? Lord, yes.

Jamie: *(quietly)* A family man, sir.

  Bill: Yeees ... They're all grown up now, flown the nest.

Jamie: Is that so, sir.

  Bill: Oh, yes. My wife ...

Jamie: Yes, sir? *(quietly)*

  Bill: Well, she used to come with me.

Jamie: I understand, sir.

  Bill: That's why we two old ones go together,
        have done for years.

Jamie: That's right, sir.

  Bill: Now, Denis – the Major,
        he's one for the fish.
        All his life,
        well, since the war.

Jamie: That's the way, sir.

  Bill: You think so?

Jamie: You were saying, sir.

Denis: Now what are you two on about,
        jabber, jabber, jabber.

  Bill: Nothing moving, Denis,
        from what I can see.

Denis: Talking doesn't help.
        You know, this is serious,
        we're not here to talk.

Jamie: That's what it is, sir.
        Many's the serious gentleman I've had with me.
        Many serious gentlemen.

  Bill: But, it's so glorious, just to be here! Right
        away from it all.

Jamie: Oh, it's away, sir. Right away.
        You couldn't get any further.

Denis: What's that you say?

  Bill: I was saying it's glorious. Cares melt.
        Just look at those mountains, even in this light.

Denis: It'll not do you much good, to stare into space.

  Bill: You can feel it all, soaking into you; so restful.

Denis: Stuff and nonsense. I'm here to catch fish.

Bill: Denis, just look round.

Denis: If I wanted to see sights, I'd be out of this boat.

Bill: Jamie, what do you think?

Jamie: Me, sir?

Bill: Yes.

Jamie: Mmm, what shall I say, sir?

Bill: Isn't it wonderful, to have this all round you?

Jamie: Well, sir, it is good to know it's there.

Bill: But what do you think?

Jamie: Think, sir... that's a question.
And, and, you see, sir, I'm not here to fish.

Denis: Absolutely. What's more, Bill, I begin to think
you're not, either. Hm! All this chatter. Impossible
to concentrate, *(to Jamie)* He talks too much.

Jamie: He's a great one for the talk, sir.

Denis: It gets in the way.

Jamie: Some people like talking, sir.

Denis: And some people never stop.

Jamie: That's a true word, sir.

Denis: I like a man who knows when to stop.

Jamie: Ah, sir, now that's a man.

Denis: You agree.

Jamie: They say silence is golden, sir.

Denis: Let's hope we can have some.
*(lights dim briefly. Jamie then stands up, turns round
and sits facing the other direction. Dialogue speeds up)*

Denis: All right, boatman, let's be getting home.

Bill: By the way, Denis,
there's something I've been wanting to ask you.

Denis: Oh, what is it? *(dialogue picks up speed again)*

Bill: D'you tie your own flies?

Denis: No, I don't tie flies.

Jamie: He doesn't tie flies.

Denis: No, actually, I've got a woman.

Bill: You've got a woman?

Jamie:	He's actually got a woman.
Denis:	Anyway, it isn't the fly.
Bill:	It isn't the fly?
Jamie:	Oh, it isn't the fly.
Denis:	It's the man behind the rod.
Bill:	The man behind the rod.
Jamie:	The what behind the rod?
Denis:	You heard.
Jamie:	You didn't.
Bill:	He never does.
Denis:	Well!
Bill:	Well.
Jamie:	Well.
Bill:	I like the mornings.
Denis:	Yes, the mornings are best.
Jamie:	I'll be damned, two mornings, one mind.
Denis / Bill:	Do you mind.
Jamie:	I most certainly do!
Denis / Bill:	It really was the weather.
Jamie:	They're like birds of a feather.
Bill:	You can't beat the weather.
Denis:	No excuses, you.
Jamie:	*(sarcastic)* I'll excuse them.
Bill:	I never mind if I don't catch anything.
Denis:	Anything?
Bill:	Anything.
Jamie:	What he's not admitting is, that he can't do anything quite as well as you.
Bill:	Not *any* thing, one thing.
Denis:	Now, that's a point of view which won't hold water.
Bill:	Won't hold what?
Jamie:	I think he said water.
Denis:	No water, please, just a little ice.
Jamie:	Now where would the likes of me, be a getting of some ice?

Denis: No, certainly no water.

Bill: Now, *that* was a fish.

Denis: What was a fish?

Bill: That first one.

Denis: You mean the one that got away. I'd say no size.

Jamie: I'd say so, too.

Bill: I felt that fish.

Jamie: He might go a pound.

Denis: A pound? If that.

Bill: Well, leave me something of the day.

Jamie: And why, when all is said and done?

Denis: Day-dreams of fish. You must be mad.

Bill: Who's mad?

Jamie: What pot and kettle have we here,
both black with dross,
one called a dream.

Denis: No time for dreams if fish you want.

Bill: No time? *You* must be mad, your latter life is just one fish.

Denis: Not one fish, fish!

Bill: Just what I mean.

Jamie: Just what they mean,
is mean as mean,
and twice as twenty times.

Bill: We've had some times.

Jamie: You've had your times all right,
and now your time is nearly up.

Bill: Another drift.

Jamie: *Another* drift!

Bill: Yes, I'd've liked another drift.

Jamie: I'd had enough.

Denis: I'd had enough.

Bill: But I'd've liked another drift.

Denis: You had your chance.

Bill: You never know.

Denis: Oh, I don't know.

Jamie: They never know.

Denis: I thought it was the time to stop.

  Bill: No more drink: that's what it was.

Jamie: That's what it was and what it is.

  Bill: And what it is, he drank my drink.

Jamie: Whisky would have wet my whistle
        smoothed the waves
        oiled my arms
        sped the blood
        raised the mind
        above the spirits
        all the way across the lake.

Denis: Can't waste that stuff;
        all these chaps do is drink and drink.

  Bill: Bet he fumbles, leaving me to pay.

Jamie: I wonder which'll give me what.

Denis: Bum-sit all day: then want a tip.
        I've no patience with that kind.

  Bill: I wonder what they think of us?

Jamie: I wonder what they think they are?

Denis: I wonder if they think we're dumb,
        these boatmen,
        arriving late: back home for tea.

  Bill: What does go on inside those minds?

Denis: What?

  Bill: God, can't you hear?

Denis: I can hear all right, you fool.

  Bill: I bet that fool can hear all right.
        (loud) I said I wonder what they think.

Jamie: You watch it.

Denis: Damn all, I'd say.
        Lazy lumpish lot: their lives asleep in boats away.

Jamie: It's hard, this seat,
        wet work, long day,
        (suddenly much slower)
        in the shrivel and cramp of a wayward wind.
        Do this, do that, with a lickspittle grin.

Bill:	What a way to spend a day.
	That Denis, why,
	I begin to think he's a bit of a scrounge.
Denis:	And what was that?
Jamie:	Your friend is right.
Denis:	Is what?
Jamie:	You idle, upper-crusted loaf.
Denis:	Speak for yourself.
Jamie:	I do and all.
Denis:	Did you speak?
Jamie:	You know I did.
Denis:	I thought a voice.
Bill:	And I did, too.
Jamie:	'tis but the sounds.
Denis:	You spoke.
Bill:	*You* spoke!
Jamie:	But I'm the one who has the ears.
Denis:	You've got a cheek.
Jamie:	Two cheeks.
Denis:	Well, turn it.
Jamie:	It's already turned,
	a brighter red than setting sun.
Bill:	What a nerve.
Jamie:	No nerve, sir.
	It doesn't pay,
	to have a nerve.
Denis:	I'll have you know.
Jamie:	Sir?
Denis:	And don't you sir me.
Jamie:	Oh but sir! You're entitled.
Denis:	A title. Now you're talking.
Bill:	Sir William sounds nice.
Denis:	We were talking of me.
Bill:	What've *you* done?
Denis:	Done? My dear chap, I *am*.
Jamie:	He certainly is.

Denis: It would go with my name.

Bill: *(giggles)* I still think Sir William would just fit the bill. I'm a terrible one.

Jamie: You what, sir?

Bill: For making a pun.

Jamie: It's a terrible pun, sir.

Denis: Now no lip from you.

Jamie: Two lips, sir.

Denis: Oh no! Not again.

Jamie: No. Last time was cheek.

Denis: It's the jolly same thing.

Jamie: But not to me.

Denis: You're a pain in the neck.

Jamie: That's just what I get,
and where I get it.
All that wind.

Denis: What wind?

Jamie: Oh, the east-north wind.
You're a bag of it.

Denis: What of it?

Jamie: Bag of it.

Bill: What was that?

Jamie: Now don't *you* start!

Bill: Oh, the bag … yes, not a bad bag.

Jamie: Two bags.

Denis: Two bags?

Jamie: Yes, *you* bags!

Denis: One bag's enough, I'll have you know.

Jamie: Oh, bugger the bag.
All I want now is home to my tea.

Denis: Tea?

Jamie: Well, if given the choice, I'd rather have beer.

Denis: Beer?

Jamie: Weeell, whisky'd be nice.

Denis: I knew it: you buggers are all the same.

Jamie: It's all the same to you.

Bill: All the same, it's a lovely rod.

Denis: I don't hold with these new-fangled fads.

Bill: Just because it's lighter than yours.

Denis: Ah, but who got the fish.

Bill: Oh! You and your fish.

Jamie: To hell with your fish.

Denis: You never could take it.

Bill: It's the luck of the take.

Jamie: Who's on about luck?

Denis: Just what would you know?
We give, and you take.

Jamie: Some take and don't give.

Denis: Now you're being childish.

Jamie: Ah, sir, the child is father of the man.

Denis: Exactly.

Jamie: Exactly.

Bill: Denis, that man's a fast one.

Jamie: You're the fast one, never a faster.
Slow and solid, there you've got me,
thick in the arm and thick in the head,
that's the way to my daily bread.

Denis: Now that reminds me.

Bill: Reminds you?

Denis: Yes, that packed lunch was a perfect disgrace.

Bill: I didn't think it was all that bad.

Jamie: It was bad for me,
since there was none for me.

Denis: Who asked you?

Jamie: Nobody.

Denis: Nobody!

Jamie: Isn't that the point.

Denis: Now, nobody.

Jamie: Nobody?

Denis: Nobody could call me a fussy man.

Jamie: Cor, bloody hell.

Denis: But there wasn't even any butter on one slice of bread.

Jamie:	There, there.
Bill:	Now, now.
Denis:	Now stoppit, stoppit, the pair of you.
Jamie:	I'm not here to stop.
Bill:	Well, what are you here for?
Jamie:	Here for?
Denis / Bill:	Yes, my good man, here for.
Jamie:	Oh, I'm here for the day, your day.
	I am your lordships' most humble and obedient.
Bill:	Do you believe that, Denis?
Denis:	No… but it's a fiction I enjoy.
	After all, we pay for what we get.
Bill:	Oh, I don't know.
Denis:	Too much!
Bill:	Too much, do you really think so?
Jamie:	Too bloody much, *(slow and ironic)*
	In fact you're much of a muchness.
Bill:	How can you say that? I was being so nice.
Jamie:	Oh, you're nice, sir, three bags full, sir.
	Your questions were pointed.
Bill:	I think this is the end.
Denis:	The end?
Bill:	The absolute end.
Jamie:	Is that your final word on the matter, sir,
	because it's fine with me.
Bill:	You misunderstand me.
Jamie:	That's right, sir.
	But I really do think we're reaching the end.
Denis:	I have certainly had more than enough.
Jamie:	I concur heartily, sir.
	Shall we just try the final chorus through
	once again.
	All together now. One, two, three.
Bill:	There's a fish….
Denis:	Where's a fish?
Jamie:	You're a fish.

Bill: He's a fish?
            (slight pause)
Bill: Here a fish.
Denis: There a fish.
Jamie: Everywhere a fish, fish.
            Old Macdonald had a f ...
Denis / Bill: Oh no!
            (lights)

Jo Rippier was born in Plymouth, went to King's School, Worcester, before studying at Emmanuel College, Cambridge. He was a lecturer at the English Department of Frankfurt University for many years, where he was much involved with drama, and where a number of his plays were performed.